LIBRARY

... with a Mission!

For Abbie, Donal and Barry, my GREAT-niece and GREAT-nephews, with love – *MF*

To Marie, Guy and Ploum, a lovely little dog who doesn't need to go to Dog School! – *JD*

STRIPES PUBLISHING
An imprint of Magi Publications
1 The Coda Centre, 189 Munster Road, London SW6 6AW

A paperback original
First published in Great Britain in 2008

Text copyright © Maeve Friel, 2008
Illustrations copyright © Joelle Dreidemy, 2008

The right of Maeve Friel and Joelle Dreidemy to be identified as the author and illustrator of this work has been asserted by them in accordance with the Copyright, Designs and Patents Act, 1988.

ISBN: 978-1-84715-040-0

A CIP catalogue record for this book is available from the British Library.

Printed and bound in Belgium

10 9 8 7 6 5 4 3 2 1

Tiger Lily

A Heroine with a Mission!

Maeve Friel

Illustrated by
Joelle Dreidemy

Stripes

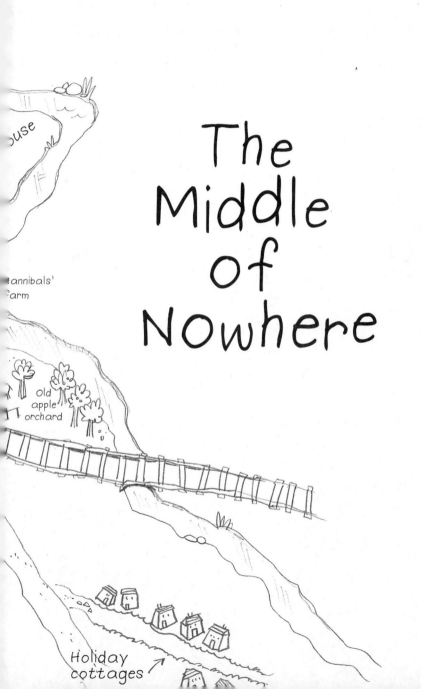

ouse

annibals'
arm

Old
apple
orchard

The
Middle
of
Nowhere

Holiday
cottages

The Visitors to The Middle of Nowhere

Sandy Marsh and the Out and About team

Mr Golightly

The Malones

The K9 Six

Lauren and Snoopy

Me and Rosie

Katy and Mitzi

Sammy and Zog

Streaky Junior and X-an

Danny and Pugsy

Chapter 1

"I could murder that peacock," said Mum, sinking into a deckchair and fanning herself with a copy of the *Daily Bugle*. Tiger Lily steered her wheelbarrow of books around the apple tree and stared at her mother.

"You can't kill peacocks, Mum – they're beautiful. And anyway, I bet they taste disgusting. You'd need loads of ketchup."

"Don't be silly, Lily. I don't want to EAT it. I mean I really want to *murder* it. It's pecking holes in all the apples and its constant 'Waaarghs' are driving me mad."

The peacock that Tiger and her mum were talking about had crashed into their apple tree earlier that morning and had been screeching ever since. It was one of the peacocks from Hannibals' Rare Breeds farm next door. They were *always* escaping. They strutted around the village streets and held up the traffic to show off their magnificent fan tails. They swaggered along the railway line without a care in the world, and ate the flowers in Smoky Bacon's hanging baskets.

"It's only screeching because it's hot too," Tiger Lily said, as she set down her wheelbarrow beside the shed. "*I'm* baking and I don't have all those feathers to drag around behind me."

It was August 1st, Operation Clear Out Day, the day that Tiger Lily and her mum, Vicky, had finally decided to do something about all the books in their house.

Books spilled out of their bookcases and marched up the stairs. They stood sentry on the windowsills and collected on the tops of wardrobes.

They squatted on the kitchen chairs, spread out over the tables and multiplied behind the curtains.

They were everywhere.

11

The problem was that Tiger Lily and her mum had never seen a book they didn't want to take home. Mum, who drove the mobile library, was always buying withdrawn library books, and Tiger Lily was always picking up second-hand books in the charity shop whenever she and her mum went to the city. Her head was so full of stories that, more than anything, she wanted to become a heroine and roam the world having exciting adventures of her own, just like the people in her books.

The only thing that stood in Tiger's way was the fact that she lived in The Middle of Nowhere, where nothing ever happened. There were no enemy pirates on the island, there was no secret staircase in the woods to lead her to an underground country and, as far as she knew, there were no tiny people living under the floorboards at home … though it might be worth a look…

But as she emptied her wheelbarrow under the watchful eye of the peacock, she made up her mind. Someday soon, somebody was going to need a heroine and she would be there, ready to take up arms, to right a wrong or solve a mystery.

"Waaargh!" screamed the peacock again as it swaggered on to the lawn. It rattled its gleaming metallic-blue tail feathers and started to raise them in a spectacular arc.

Lily and her mum turned around to watch. They weren't the only ones.

13

Rosie, Tiger's three-legged greyhound, was watching it too. Her nose twitched. She crept out from under the garden bench, raised herself on her haunches and carefully steadied herself, ready to run.

"Quick, Lily! Grab her collar," Mum screamed.

It was too late. Rosie took off.

The peacock looked over its shoulder, squawked and broke into an awkward run, dragging its tail behind it.

"Quick! Do something!" Mum yelled. "Don't let the dog kill the peacock. It's

probably worth a fortune!"

"ROSIE!" Tiger yelled. "STOP! SIT! STAY! HEEL!"

Rosie paid absolutely no attention.

She bounded excitedly across the grass with the peacock in her sights.

Lily broke into a fast run.

"Get her, Tiger!" shouted Mum.

Tiger Lily grinned, for her mum hardly ever called her Tiger.

She hurled herself at Rosie in a spectacular flying tackle, just as Rosie rose up on her hind legs to leap on the bird.

They crash-landed together on the peacock's tail.

The bird gave a furious squawk, wiggled itself free and clumsily took off in a low flight over the garden wall.

Rosie was left sitting on three beautiful feathers with emerald-green eyes.

Mum let out a very long, deep breath. "What were you saying about a new Dog School last night?" she asked.

"Oh Mum, can I do it, please? It's at Hannibals' farm. And the best thing is there's a special course for children. I've got the flyer in my book."

Tiger Lily never went anywhere without her special book where she wrote her diary and her book reports and made drawings and kept other useful stuff.

"Let's have a look," said Mum.

16

IS YOUR DOG GOING TO THE DOGS?

Does your dog pull at his lead
or run off without warning?
Does he refuse to obey your
orders? Does he barge through
doors? Jump up at people?
Chase other dogs? Does he chew
inappropriate objects? Does he
bark when left alone? Does he
have toilet accidents?
If you have answered
'yes' to any of these, you need
K9 Coaching.
To celebrate the opening of our
Dog School, we are offering a
FUN-FILLED DOG TRAINING COURSE
for children and their dogs.
Enrolment Friday, 3-5pm
Hannibals' Farm.

"Is there anything here you don't need to tick?" asked Mum. "Well, she doesn't chase other dogs."

"Maybe not," agreed Mum. "But don't peacocks count? Or cats – remember when she went after all the cats in Sweetness and Light's shop?"

Tiger Lily winced. "Yes, but that was an unfortunate—"

Mum held up a hand. "No excuses. Look, I would let you go to Dog School if I thought Rosie's behaviour would improve, but face it, Lily, she's crackers. We don't know what sort of life she had before you found her. She really HAS TO GO before you start back at school. She would be much better off in a home for retired greyhounds."

18

Tiger Lily bit her lip. "Please, Mum…"

Mum sighed. "And you know that Mrs Hannibal is a complete grouch, don't you? It mightn't be as much fun as you think."

"Please, Mum, at least let me try."

Mum fanned herself with the leaflet. "Oh Lily, you're impossible! All right, but remember – if Rosie's behaviour doesn't improve big time by the end of the month, she HAS TO GO."

"Oh thank you, thank you, thank you." Lily gave her mum a big hug. "I'm sure Rosie will be the best in the class." Over her shoulder she could see Rosie tucking into Mum's newspaper. She gave her a hard warning stare. Rosie paid no attention.

From the other side of the river, the 13:25 train gave a long, low whistle as it crossed the railway bridge.

Lily's eyes lit up. "Oh, Mum, that's Sammy's train."

Sammy was Lily's best friend although they only met up when he came to stay with his dad during half-terms and holidays. No one could imagine two less likely best friends. Lily was always having Big Ideas; Sammy was sensible and down to earth. She loved reading; he never read if he could help it. He was a very good drummer; she couldn't tell a hi-hat from a crash cymbal.

She had a lot of springy red and gold hair – that's why everyone called her Tiger; Sammy had hardly any hair at all.

"Maybe Sammy might like to go to Dog School as well with his spaniel wotsisname?"

"With Zog? Oh Mum, that's a brilliant idea. Can I go and meet him and bring him back for lunch, and then we'll go to the Hannibals together?"

"Okay, but," Lily's mum waggled her fingers at the three peacock feathers, "promise you won't say a word to anyone about those, Lily? I don't want Mrs Hannibal barging in here shouting 'I PROTEST' and telling everyone that we are attacking her animals."

Lily giggled. "Cross my heart," she said. She picked up the feathers, rushed into the house, threw them on her bed and grabbed the surprise banner she had made for Sammy.

"Back in a minute," she shouted. "Come on, Rosie."

Chapter 2

When Tiger and Rosie arrived at the station, the train was just pulling in. Smoky Bacon, the stationmaster, was trotting along the platform looking at the watch he kept in his waistcoat pocket and wiping his forehead with a large handkerchief. Unusually, that afternoon there were a lot of passengers, for it was the start of the summer holidays. Several families struggled down the steps with pushchairs and holdalls and rucksacks and babies and golf bags and fishing rods. One of them had a very yappy pug.

TIGERLILY

Next to appear was a giant stranger who came scowling out of the guard's van, wheeling a bike. "So this is The Middle of Nowhere," he muttered, as he handed his ticket to Smoky, "twinned, I have no doubt, with The Back of Beyond and The Far Side of the Moon."

Smoky bristled with indignation. "As a

matter of fact, sir, some of us regard our village as The Centre of the Universe, isn't that right, Tiger?"

But before Tiger had time to reply, she heard a familiar bark and Zog came running up behind her, with Sammy grinning and waving a new bow and arrow. Nick the Chippie trundled after them.

Tiger Lily ran forward, holding aloft her homemade sign:

Welcome home My Trusty Companion!

Sammy's smile vanished. He groaned.

"Oh no, Tiger! Do I still have to do that? I mean, be your Trusty Companion?"

"Of course," said Lily, beaming. "Every heroine has to have one. And besides, you promised, remember? On Midsummer Night."

Sammy turned bright red. He had been trying to forget all the things that had gone wrong since Lily had made him her Trusty Companion. First she turned him into a slave called Jim and made him sail down the river

on a raft made out of a pallet. That got him grounded. Then his pocket money was stopped when Rosie and Zog attacked all the cats in the post office. And then, as if that wasn't bad enough, Lily had tricked him into playing a fairy called Puck in *A Midsummer Night's Dream* – he had had to wear bright-green tights and wings and a ridiculous hat!

"I will only be your Trusty Companion again, Tiger," he said, "on one condition. I am NEVER dressing up like an idiot ever, ever again and, secondly, you have to buy me a hi-hat if you get me into any more trouble."

"That's two conditions, and why do you want a high hat if you don't like dressing up?"

Nick the Chippie laughed. "Come on, let's go. I want to pick up my rod and get

27

down to the river before all these tourists take my fish. Do you guys want to come over to the island with me?"

Nick liked to fish on a little island in the middle of the river. There were stepping stones over to it and a small hut on the gravelly beach where he sat, with his rod stuck in the pebbles, drinking tea.

Tiger shook her head. "No thanks," she said, "because Mum's invited Sammy for lunch, and then we're going to Hannibals' farm. Mrs Hannibal has started a Dog School called K9 Coaching…"

…And before they had even reached the end of the platform, she had forgotten her promise and told them how Rosie had just yanked three feathers out of one of the Hannibals' peacocks.

28

The first thing that Tiger Lily noticed when she and Sammy turned into One-End Street was the smell of burning. A white plume of smoke was rising in a straight column from behind her house.

"Mum!"

Lily and Rosie barged through the front door with Sammy and Zog at their heels.

"Mum?" Lily yelled again. "What's burning?"

She hurtled along the hall, past the boxes of unsorted books and bundles of colour supplements, and pulled open the back door.

Mum was standing beside a bonfire, feeding it with books.

"Mum, what are you doing?" Lily spluttered. "You cannot burn books! It's a crime against humanity! A denial of free speech! You are destroying a treasury of human knowledge! Isn't that what you always say?"

"Calm down, Lily! I'm not burning books. I'm getting rid of rubbish."

Lily looked at the flames creeping around the edges of curling pages and the cinder-grey papers disintegrating into ashes.

"You see? They're just old bills and college notes and—"

"Books!" Lily pounced. "Look! *The Onion Grower's Guide to Pests and Disease*!"

Her mum raised an eyebrow. "You want to read that?"

"Well, what about this?" Lily picked up a partly-scorched magazine that had blown off to the side and read the front cover.

"Wow! I don't believe it!" She was so

31

surprised she plopped down on the deckchair.

"What is it?" said Sammy and Mum.

"It's all about Astrid Lindgren, the person who wrote *Pippi Longstocking*."

"What about her?" said Mum.

"Who's P. P. Lungs Talking?" asked Sammy.

"Sammy!" Lily snorted. "How can you NOT know about Pippi Longstocking?"

Tiger Lily's Book Reports
As Told to her trusty companion, Sammy.

Pippi Longstocking by Astrid Lindgren

Pippi Longstocking is a mad girl who lives all by herself in a cottage with a pet horse and a monkey called Mr Nelson. When she was younger, she travelled all over the world with her father until he was blown into the sea.

The best thing about Pippi is that she can do anything she wants - she even strands two policemen on her roof when they come to take her to an Institution — that's like a prison for children, I think. She has a bag of gold coins to pay for anything she needs and she is so strong she can LIFT her horse. She has two Trusty Companions called Annika and Tommy and they LOVE her because she makes their life more exciting.

This is one of my best books.

I give it: 5 big Mr Nelson smiling faces

TIGERLILY

"So, you see," Tiger Lily turned to her mum, "you can't burn this magazine until I've read it. It's probably very important."

"Lily, this is supposed to be Operation Clear Out Day."

"I know, Mum, I promise I won't keep anything else, just this."

From the top of the apple tree, the peacock let out a deafening screech.

"Waaargh! Waaargh!"

"Is that the same bird Rosie pulled the tail feathers off?" asked Sammy.

"Lily!" protested Mum. "How could you? You promised."

34

While Mum was making lunch, Tiger Lily wrote out part of a poem with peacocks and tigers in it and stuck it on the fridge.

Tartary by Walter de la Mare

If I were Lord of Tartary
Myself, and me alone,
My bed should be of ivory,
Of beaten gold my throne;
And in my court should PEACOCKS flaunt,
And in my forests TIGERS haunt,
And in my pools great FISHES slant
Their fins athwart the sun.

"If I really was the Lord of Tartary," said Tiger, grandly, "then I would reward you for being my Devoted Mother. You could have your own palace with your own peacocks and tigers – and trumpeters to play for you at mealtimes."

"That sounds far too hot and noisy," said Mum, fanning herself with the K9 Coaching leaflet. "I don't want my own peacocks and tigers! And definitely no trumpeters. I'd prefer somewhere cold and quiet with penguins and polar bears."

"Your wish is my command," said Tiger. "And Sammy, you can be the Governor of my islands."

"Cool," said Sammy, "being a governor sounds better than being a Trusty Companion."

36

"But now, Your Excellencies," said Mum, "we'd better go. I'll take you down to the Hannibals before my driving lesson."

"But you can drive already," said Sammy.

"Yes, but I need a special licence to drive a new type of library lorry, and if I don't pass the test I will have to work in the City Library with my Awful Boss—"

"And that," interrupted Tiger, "would be a Fate Worse Than Death."

Chapter 3

Electra and Fergus Hannibal had arrived in The Middle of Nowhere a year earlier. Everyone could see that they were not ordinary farmers. In fact, they weren't really farmers at all. They had been teachers for years and years and years, but they had always dreamed of having their own Rare Breeds farm.

First they got a herd of Highland cattle with long, wavy hair and the kind of enormous horns that important Viking chiefs had on their helmets. Mr Hannibal was

hoping to sell their beef to all the best hotels and restaurants, but he wasn't quite sure how to go about it.

They also kept angora goats so that Mrs Hannibal could make goat's cheese and knit soft scarves and baby blankets, but, as it turned out, Mrs Hannibal wasn't any good at knitting and she hated the goats. They kicked over their milk buckets and went on walkabouts, tripping in line across the railway bridge, breaking into people's gardens and *twice* eating an entire washing line of Auntie Pamela's towels.

Then they started to breed ornamental India Blue peacocks to sell as pets to rich people with big gardens. But the peahens kept hiding their eggs, and the neighbours complained about the noise of the peacocks. Their dream was rapidly turning into a nightmare. They needed to come up with some new ideas, fast.

That was why Mrs Hannibal, who was great with dogs, had decided to start up K9 Coaching…

…And that very afternoon, Mr Hannibal had arrived back from an agricultural show with *his* latest idea to turn their fortunes around. It was in a crate in the yard, waiting to be moved to its new home.

Lily and Sammy peered through the slats while they waited for Mrs Hannibal to come back with the K9 Coaching Register.

It was a sort of a pig. It had a thick, rough coat of reddish-brown hair, with a ridge of longer hair standing up all along its back. It had a long narrow snout, and two upturned fangs that made it look both goofy and dangerous.

"She's called Ermina," boomed Mrs Hannibal as she came out of the farmhouse. "She's a wild boar. Fergus says wild boar meat is the new ostrich."

41

At the sound of a human voice, Ermina rose on to her sturdy feet. Her snout quivered. She gave the walls of her crate a mighty kick and a headbutt for good measure.

Tiger Lily and Sammy took a step back. "She looks very, er, interesting…" said Tiger.

"…and very, um, wild," said Sammy.

Mrs Hannibal pursed her lips. "I daresay she just wants to stretch her legs after the long journey. Fergus will move her into the meadow once he's fixed the fencing."

Ermina gave the wall another fierce kick which triggered a hullabaloo of high-pitched squealing and squeaking deep inside the crate.

Tiger Lily peeped through the slats again. Sheltering underneath Ermina and tumbling over each other were six piglets.

They did not look like their mother.

Nor did they look like the usual sort of bald, pink piglets.

Ermina's babies had light-brown and cream stripes from their noses to the end of their tails.

"They look like they're wearing pyjamas," Tiger Lily said.

"They look like little grilled sausages," Sammy said.

Ermina looked down her long snout and gave her crate another fierce thump.

Tiger Lily and Sammy jumped back again.

"Come along," said Mrs Hannibal, briskly, "let's leave Ermina and her boarlets in peace."

She turned to look at Rosie – who had chosen that particular moment to try and sniff Mrs Hannibal's bottom. "Down, Tiger, down!" she roared.

Tiger Lily threw herself to the ground.

Mrs Hannibal looked at her, astonished. "What *are* you doing?"

"You told me to get down."

"No, I didn't. I was talking to Tiger."

"I am Tiger. My dog is called Rosie."

"Of course it is," said Mrs Hannibal, not listening. "Now get up and don't be silly. Tell me, how did Tiger lose her leg?"

Sammy snorted with laughter.

Mrs Hannibal gave him a withering look. "You, young man, had better buck up your ideas. I can see that Zog isn't getting anything like enough exercise. And nor are you, by the look of things." She snapped the top off a pen and wrote their names down in her book. "Now off you go. Here comes Fergus with the trailer to move Ermina to the lower meadow. See you here at nine o'clock on the dot tomorrow morning. Bring a pocketful of dog biscuits."

And she shooed them down the farm avenue.

Chapter 4

"I don't know if I want to do this dog training, Tiger," Sammy said, as they turned on to the main road. "Hatchet-face Hannibal is barking mad."

"But K9 Coaching is my last chance to keep Rosie," Tiger explained. "Otherwise, Mum is sending her to some awful place for mad dogs – it's an INSTITUTION, Sammy! Rosie would die of a broken heart. We have to save her."

"But why do *I* have to do the training?"

"Because you're my Trusty Companion, silly."

Sammy groaned. "I just want to play my drums and practise with my new bow and arrow. And I especially do not want to have to get up for nine o'clock on Saturday and Sunday mornings."

"Please, Sammy, please, please, please."

As Sammy dithered, a cyclist swooshed past them in a streak of sleek black lycra and a fancy aerodynamic helmet.

ZZZZ OOOOOOM

Moments later, Ermina crashed over the Hannibals' farm gate and darted out on to the road. A string of squealing boarlets squeezed under the gate and ran after her.

"Wow!" screamed Lily and Sammy together. "Wow! Ermina has escaped!"

The cyclist saw the wild boar and swerved into the other side of the road.

An oncoming car sounded its horn.

Ermina stopped dead. The leading boarlet collided into her backside. The rest scattered in all directions.

The car driver veered to the right, overcorrected and veered to the left. The car horn blared.

One small boarlet dodged between Rosie's back legs. Rosie barked. Zog barked. Sammy screamed and Lily screamed, but they both managed to keep a tight hold of their dogs' leads.

The motorist slammed on his brakes. The cyclist teetered and wobbled and, in slow motion, toppled off and rolled himself into a tight ball.

Ermina sniffed the air. Her nostrils flared. She glared from the cyclist to the car to the dogs. Long sticky gloops of drool dribbled from her fangs. Finally, she grunted a sharp command that brought all her terrified boarlets into line. Then she did a U-turn and charged back over the gate with her stripy family running behind her, trampling over the cyclist and his bike.

Sammy and Lily ran to pick him up.

"What sort of crazy place is this?" the cyclist groaned.

"I HATE and ABOMINATE the countryside." He unfolded himself like a jack-in-the-box, and stood up.

It was the giant stranger who had been so rude at the railway station.

"What's crazy about it?" Tiger Lily protested.

"What!" spluttered the man. "I could have been killed by that beast. This poor man," he added, pointing at the driver of the car, "could have been killed."

The driver got out. It was Spanners Murphy, their friend the cowboy plumber.

"Howdy-doody, Tiger. Y'all back for the holidays, Sammy?" He pushed his hat to the back of his head and gave the front wheel of the bike a friendly kick. "At least you've only got a crooked wheel, not a crooked leg," he drawled.

"I'm going to call the police," said the cyclist, unamused. "I'm going to have that animal's owner arrested. This is a SCANDAL and a DISGRACE."

"NO, NO!" shouted Tiger Lily, far too loudly. "There's no need for that."

The last thing she wanted was for the Hannibals to be arrested. Then there would be no Dog School and Mum would say that Rosie HAD TO GO.

"Oh yes there is," he huffed. "There must be a law about this sort of thing. You can't have animals gallivanting on the public highway."

Tiger Lily tilted her head to look up at him. He was the tallest and thinnest person she had ever seen.

"Perhaps Sammy's dad could fix your wheel for you. He's very good at fixing things. And you could have a cup of coffee in my granny's café while you're waiting. She makes very good cake."

"She does indeed," said Spanners, helpfully.

"Cake? Do I look like the sort of person who eats cake?" the Big Unfriendly Giant blustered.

Tiger drew herself up to her full height. "If you don't like the countryside, why have you come here?"

For a moment, it looked as if the man was not going to answer.

"If you must know," he said, "I'm not supposed to be here at all. I'm supposed to be in the Caribbean in a five-star luxury golf resort, but there was a mix-up and they sent Lightfoot from the Sports page there instead of me. So now I am cycling around The

Middle of Nowhere doing Lightfoot's assignment, and he is having a ball at Golf World with Tiger Woods. And what's worse, I'm staying in a bed and breakfast run by a mad opera freak above a hairdressing salon that stinks of lavender! Me! Julius Golightly – The *Daily Bugle*'s premier travel writer!"

Tiger Lily's mouth dropped open. Sammy's mouth dropped open. Spanners Murphy held up a hand. "Now, hold it right there, mister, you're talking about this girl's Auntie Pamela, one of the finest women in—"

Mr Golightly cut him off. "The Middle of Nowhere, I know." He turned to Tiger. "Now, get that pathetic excuse of a dog out of my way. I'm going to give this farmer a piece of my mind."

And he hobbled off towards the farm

with his bike going ker-plunk, ker-plunk, ker-plunk beside him.

"What a horrible man!" Tiger Lily exploded. "He insulted my Auntie Pamela. He insulted my dog! He insulted The Middle of Nowhere!"

"Yeah," agreed Sammy, "but did you see how that boar jumped over the gate? That was fantastic!"

Chapter 5

When they got back to Tiger Lily's, there was a note stuck on the fridge door:

Back soon.
Granny and Pam
are coming at 5.
Love Mum x

It was five to five.

Lily stuck two slices of bread in the toaster and started to read the magazine she had saved from the bonfire. "Listen here,

Sammy," she said. "It says here that Astrid Lindgren, the person who wrote *Pippi Longstocking*, had a MISSION. She made the government in Sweden change the law about farm animals. *Every pig has the right to a happy pig life* – that was her slogan."

"Didn't Swedish pigs have happy lives, then?" asked Sammy.

Tiger Lily's brow wrinkled. "Well, it sounds like the farmers used to keep chickens and pigs and things in cages that were SO small they couldn't even turn around or flap their wings."

"The pigs couldn't flap their wings?" Sammy laughed.

57

"That's not funny. Do you want marmalade or jam? So they passed a new law called Lex Astrid – Lex is the Latin for law, you know – and now nobody is allowed to lock up cattle and pigs and hens and treat them as if they were criminals."

"They still end up in bacon sandwiches and burger buns, though."

"I know, Sammy, but that's not the point. The point is, *every pig has the right to a happy pig life.* While they're alive. Or there's peanut butter?" She offered him the jar. "If you ask me, I think that *every dog has the right to a happy dog life,* and that includes Rosie. That would be my law, Lex Tiger Lily."

She imagined herself in a judge's wig and gown, pronouncing her new law to a courtroom full of cheering dogs. "I'm going to write it out and stick it on the fridge for Mum to see."

"Yoo-hoo," shouted a voice. "Anyone home?"

Granny Rita click-clacked into the kitchen. "So now you're eating like horses?"

"Hello, Granny. What do you mean, eating like horses?"

"Horses eat standing up," said Granny. "Civilized human beings sit down to eat. And they use plates."

Lily rolled her eyes. Grannies in books were always older and greyer and QUIETER than her Granny Rita. And they certainly didn't wear big earrings and high heels and bright red lipstick.

Auntie Pamela came in behind her.

"Hi, Tiger. Welcome back, Sammy." She moved a stack of books off a chair and sat down. "You'll never believe what just happened to one of my guests, Mr Golightly. He's here to write an article about bike trails around The Middle of Nowhere…"

"We know him," Lily interrupted, "and he's the most horrible man I have ever met."

"How can you say that?" protested Auntie Pamela. "He's charming and he has a lovely tenor voice. He's famous, you know – Julius Golightly of the *Daily Bugle*."

"He's not at all nice, Auntie Pamela. If you only knew," Tiger Lily said vehemently, "and he nearly killed the Hannibals' new wild boar and all her boarlets."

"Tiger, that's not really…" Sammy began.

"What he told the *police*," Auntie Pamela said, miffed that her news was not new news, "was that a herd of raging boars leaped over a farm gate and charged at him and wrecked his bike and that the Hannibals were EXTREMELY unhelpful when he complained about it…"

Tiger Lily gasped. "He told the police? Have the Hannibals been arrested?"

"No," said Auntie Pamela, "but they

61

probably ought to be. We certainly don't want wild boars RAMPAGING about The Middle of Nowhere. The goats are bad enough. Mr Golightly is going to write an article about it in the *Daily Bugle*. And he's phoning that woman on the radio, the one you like, Mum. They were at college together, apparently."

Granny Rita looked out of the window as if checking for rampaging boars. "I've heard that wild boar is very tasty," she remarked to no one in particular. "But, Tiger, here comes your mum. You'd better get that mutt of yours off the sofa on the double."

Tiger Lily's Diary

Friday evening

Today was quite an exciting day. Sammy came. We saw a wild boar and met a Big Unfriendly Giant, a BUG, called Mr Golightly. He insulted my dog and my auntie so I am glad that Ermina and her boarlets wrecked his bike.

I have read nearly all of 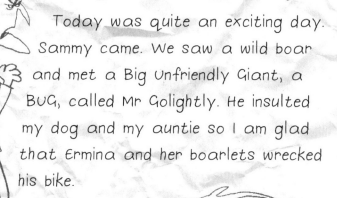 my library book, Fattypuffs and Thinifers, because I cannot sleep. I am so excited about the dog training classes. I have a new mission – I must stop Rosie from being sent away to an Institution.

LEX TIGER LILY – Every dog has the right to a happy dog life.

K9 Coaching Children's Dog Training School at Hannibals' Rare Breeds Farm

REGISTER

NAME	BREED	OWNER
X-an	German shepherd	Streaky Bacon, Jr
Pugsy	pug	Danny Malone
Snoopy	beagle	Lauren Schultz
Mitzi	poodle	Katy Carroll
Luna	bloodhound	Milo Hannibal
~~Tiger~~ Rosie	greyhound	Lily ~~Rose~~ Larkin
Zog	cocker spaniel??	Sammy Norton

Chapter 6

For anyone who liked quiet, Hannibals' farmyard was not the place to be on Saturday morning at 9am.

There were only six children and their six dogs, but they were making such a din that even Mrs Hannibal was struggling to make herself heard. The screeching of the peacocks on the barn roof didn't help.

"Streaky Bacon Junior and..." she peered at her list, "how do you pronounce your dog's name?"

"X-an, you know, like eggs and bacon."

Mrs Hannibal, vast in a green body warmer and leggings, shot a furious look at everyone to stop the tittering.

"Get in line, Streaky. And be brisk about it – I don't want to see any slouching."

Streaky Junior, a boy of about thirteen with bad skin and the beginnings of a small black moustache, oozed bad attitude.

"Come on, come on," bellowed Mrs Hannibal. "We haven't got all day. Now where are Pugsy and Danny? Put your dog down on the ground, Danny – you can't carry him around like that all day, hugging your pug as if you were a Chinese emperor."

Danny was a small, pale boy with a scattering of freckles on his

cheekbones. Pugsy was the teeny little pug with a comically squashed face and a very loud yap that Tiger Lily had seen at the railway station the day before.

"I think he's a bit scared of the other dogs," said Danny, almost in a whisper.

Tiger Lily nudged Sammy. "Who's that? Do you know him?"

"No, but I saw him on the train. He has millions of sisters and cousins just like him. His dad told my dad they're all staying in Streaky Bacon's holiday cottages," Sammy whispered back.

"EXCUSE ME FOR BREAKING UP YOUR LITTLE CHAT," Mrs Hannibal suddenly roared, making Sammy and Lily jump to attention, "but some of us have a JOB to do."

"Sorry," said Sammy and Lily together, and they turned a little pink.

"Danny, get your pug in line behind X-an, and let's have Snoopy and Lauren…"

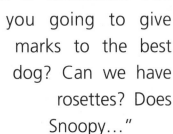

Lauren was a couple of years younger than Tiger and Sammy. She was a total chatterbox, with a permanent eager-to-please smile.

"Mrs Hannibal," she gushed, "will we get a certificate? Are you going to give marks to the best dog? Can we have rosettes? Does Snoopy…"

Mrs Hannibal cut her off. "Behind the pug, please, Lauren."

Lauren's best friend, Katy Carroll, didn't even wait for her name to be called.

"I'm Katy, Mrs Hannibal, and this is my poodle Mitzi. She's very well behaved, but she doesn't like walking on wet grass."

68

Mitzi was the most ridiculous dog that Tiger Lily had ever seen. She had white balls of puff on her legs, a silly hair-do, a pompom at the end of her tail and was wearing a jacket with a pattern of bright red hearts. Katy had a lot of pompoms, too, and was wearing a pair of pink ballet shoes.

"We'll soon cure Mitzi of that nonsense, Katy," Mrs Hannibal barked. "Poodles were bred for retrieving birds in wet marshy ground, not for sashaying around like silly supermodels. Now get in line, chop chop."

Tiger Lily and Sammy exchanged a look.

"I wonder when the fun-filled part is going to start," Sammy whispered.

Unfortunately, Mrs Hannibal heard him.

"Fancy yourself as the class clown, do you, Sammy? Well, I won't stand for it. You're the boy with the fat spaniel, aren't you? Well, let's see you do two circuits of the farmyard, NOW, and look lively." Streaky Junior tittered. Mrs Hannibal silenced him with an evil stare.

"And finally, Tiger and Rosie. Did I ask you before if you knew how Tiger lost her leg?"

"I'm Tiger," said Tiger Lily, patiently. "Rosie is my dog's name. And no, I don't know. She was like that when I found her."

"An abandoned racer, I suppose. Should be well used to training. Right, if you've all got your dog biscuits, we can begin! MILO! BRING OUT OUR DOGS!"

Milo was the Hannibals' youngest son. He was Streaky's best friend and, like him, was usually up to no good, hanging out at the swings in the playground, clattering around on a skateboard or spraying PEACOCKS ROCK on the station walls. But, like his mother, he was an expert on dogs. He came out of the farmhouse with two scary-looking dogs running alongside him on leads.

"This is Dora, my Dobermann pinscher," Mrs Hannibal shouted above X-an's belligerent barking and Pugsy's terrified yapping. "She's the pack leader, so she won't stand for any nonsense – and, as most of you know, this is my son Milo and his bloodhound, Luna."

71

"Short for lunatic," Streaky sniggered.

"You can wipe that smile off your face, Streaky," Mrs Hannibal barked. "I'll be the one to judge if there are any lunatics around here. Now, lead on, Milo, and take everyone to the apple orchard."

The children and their dogs followed Milo in a tangle of crossed leads, sudden dashes for freedom and a LOT of barking.

Danny turned very pale when they passed the meadow where Ermina was rooting for worms and her stripy boarlets were play-fighting, bouncing off each other's shoulders.

"Look!" he stammered, clutching Pugsy to his chest, "there are wild animals in that field."

"Yeah," smirked Streaky. "Wild boar – there're MILLIONS of them around here. One time I was swimming down beside the cottages where you're staying and a huge one came after me. He was as big as a hippopotamus."

"Don't worry, Danny," said Milo, slapping him on the back, "you'll be OK as long as you stay out of the water."

Danny looked as if he might burst into tears.

"Actually," said Tiger Lily, gently, "they're the only boars in the neighbourhood, and I don't think they can swim."

"For goodness sake, Tiger," said Sammy, "they don't need to SWIM to go up and down the river. Even those little striped porkers would hardly be up to their knees." He turned to Danny. "But you should see the way they can leap over fences."

Danny looked green.

When they had all finally got through the gate into the orchard, Mrs Hannibal yelled at them to line up in two rows opposite one another. Everybody had to stand with their dog beside an apple tree.

On one side there was Streaky with X-an, Tiger Lily with Rosie, Sammy with Zog and Danny with Pugsy. Opposite them were Milo with Luna, Katy with Mitzi, Lauren with Snoopy and Mrs Hatchet-face Hannibal with Dora the Dobermann.

All morning Mrs Hannibal walked up and down, barking instructions at them and blowing a whistle.

"SIT! STAY! STAND! REWARD YOUR DOG! FACE YOUR DOG! WALK AROUND YOUR DOG! SIT! STAY!"

After a bit, it WAS fun-filled, despite Hatchet-face.

Quite soon, they had learned to walk their dogs on the lead and slalom between the trees. The worst part was when they had to change places with the person at the tree opposite.

X-an – who was only a big puppy even if he was a German shepherd – didn't understand the rules of the pack and wanted to be the boss. Every time he crossed paths with Luna, he snarled and tried to go for Luna's throat.

Pugsy cringed and widdled and covered his eyes with his paws at the sight of Dora the Dobermann walking towards him.

Mitzi hated walking on grass and refused to budge even when Katy called her Mitizikins and *pulled* and *pulled*.

Zog and Snoopy the beagle just wanted to play and run around in circles, chasing each other's tails.

Rosie was really good and did as she was told most of the time, but she did like to chase after things. Mostly rooks, but once, unfortunately, Mitzi. Katy cried and wanted to go home until Tiger Lily promised to give her a great book about a poodle princess, just like Mitzi.

Tiger was so thrilled when Mrs Hannibal told everyone that greyhounds could see up to half a mile away and run at speeds of up to forty miles per hour that she told her about Lex Tiger Lily.

Mrs Hannibal thumped her on the back. "Attagirl!" she barked.

It was all very exciting.

Then Mrs Hannibal's mobile rang. "Fergus, I'm too busy to talk," she

brayed into the phone. "WHAT? I can't hear you, you're breaking up. Ermina? She's WHERE? What? The library van? The SAME cyclist? Omigod! I'm on my way!" She snapped the phone shut.

"Everyone back to their tree. That includes you too, Streaky. And Katy, stop blubbing. They're only grass stains. You can give Mitzi a bath when you get home. Milo, take over till I get back."

Tiger Lily's Diary

Saturday afternoon

I LOVE Dog School - but we had to stop early because Ermina escaped again, just when the BUG was wheeling his bike past the farm on his way to the garage. Mum had parked the library van on the main road and Sweetness and Light were changing their library books when Ermina came crashing over the gate and ran into the side of the van. There is quite a big bash and the bookstand with all the Large Print books fell over on top of one of the twins. Light - or maybe it was Sweetness - had to have a big plaster on her nose.

The Hannibals have invited them for supper at the Bay Tree Cafe to make up and then they invited all of the K9 Coaching class as well because our class was cut short. Mum says that is called a "public relations exercise". Mr Golightly turned down their invitation.

LEX TIGER LILY! Every dog has the right to a happy dog life!

Chapter 7

"Please be nice to the Wolves, Tiger," said Mum, as they walked down to the Post Office to pick up Sweetness and Light. "They've had a bit of a shock."

"Don't worry, Mum," Tiger grinned, "you can count on me. I'll be as sweet and light as can be, and so will Rosie."

Sweetness and Light took ages to get ready. By the time they took off their aprons and changed their hats and powdered their very long noses and locked up the shop and then went back to put the cats out, Mum

81

was ready to tear her hair out, and by the time they reached the café, Granny had given away all the outdoor tables in the square to tourists and they had to eat inside. It was really hot. Mum made Lily leave Rosie snoozing under the bay tree.

Sweetness and Light, sharp elbows clacking like pistons, cleared a path through a big group of people who were waiting for a table.

They were all different versions of Danny Malone, bigger and smaller and older and younger, but all with the same freckled cheekbones.

Tiger Lily squeezed in beside Sammy and his dad at the table by the window. Lauren and Katy were at the next table with their parents and Auntie Pamela was whizzing about serving, and singing 'La donna è mobile'.

All the Bacon family and Spanners Murphy were there too. Streaky Junior was dribbling all the salt in the salt cellar into the sugar bowl.

Granny's favourite phone-in programme *Out and About with Sandy Marsh* was on the radio.

"Any day now, Sandy," a whingeing voice was saying, "there will be a bloodbath, make no mistake about it. These wild boar farms must be banned."

"I recognize that *lovely tenor* voice," said Tiger Lily, poking Sammy in the ribs. "Look! It's the Big Unfriendly Giant."

Outside in the square, they could see the BUG strutting around with his mobile clamped to his ear.

His disembodied voice whined on. "My top-of-the-range bike is a write-off, the library van is wrecked and two elderly women are in a state of shock. One of them has had to have medical treatment..."

"Elderly? How rude!" Sweetness exploded (or it might have been Light – it was the one who didn't have the X of sticking-plasters on her nose).

"I ask you!" said Light (or it might have been Sweetness – it was the one with the sticking plasters). "Do we look old to you?"

Everyone suddenly became very busy stirring and cutting and chewing and fishing under the tables for their napkins.

In the silence, Danny's dad coughed

85

politely. "Excuse me, Miss," he said to Auntie Pamela, "could you tell me if Mr Bacon is here tonight?"

Auntie Pamela gave him a charming smile. "They're both here. Take your pick, Smoky or Streaky."

On hearing his name, Streaky Bacon Senior half-turned around, which was not such an easy thing to do for he was like a spacehopper wedged on a chair between the wall and the table.

Danny's dad murmured something that Tiger Lily couldn't hear, but the next thing, Streaky struggled out of his seat and draped a massive arm around Mr Malone's tiny shoulders.

"Why on earth would you want your money back?" he laughed unconvincingly. "Just because of some teensy-weensy boars."

Everyone turned around.

86

The Malone family looked terrified to be the centre of so much attention.

Mum took pity on them. "A wild boar isn't teensy, Streaky," she said. "I can tell you a boar weighing hundreds of kilos charging blindly into the side of your van and knocking over your Large Print section is no laughing matter."

"You can say that again," said Sweetness (or Light), pointing at her sister's long nose.

"You should claim compensation," Spanners Murphy drawled in his mock American accent. "The library—"

"Can we PLEASE have a bit of shush," said Mum, snapping a breadstick in two as if she was breaking the neck of a small animal. "I'm trying to hear if he says anything about me…"

As Mum was speaking, Tiger spotted the Hannibals driving up in their jeep. Mr Hannibal got out, talking into his mobile, while Mrs Hannibal went off to park.

He sat down on the bench beside the bay tree, deliberately ignoring Mr Golightly, who was still pacing angrily up and down between the café and the Old Jam Factory.

Everyone in the café jumped when the farmer's voice suddenly boomed over the radio.

88

"...let your listeners know that boars are really very shy creatures that wouldn't say boo to a goose..."

"Hah!" snorted Mum. "Try telling that to my Awful Boss."

"...and they are all safely padlocked in my barn while we are working flat out on reinforcing the fences."

"That's not good enough, Mr Hannibal," Sandy Marsh snapped. "My very good friend, Julius Golightly, a journalist of INTERNATIONAL renown, could have been killed this afternoon..."

"Now, Sandy," Mr Hannibal said in a really smarmy voice, "I want you to know that since this unfortunate incident—"

"This SECOND incident," interrupted Mr Golightly in his self-important voice. "Frankly, Mr Hannibal, I put it to you, sir, that you are a BLOCKHEAD and an IGNORAMUS when it comes to farming."

There was a sharp intake of breath in the café. Everyone looked out of the window to see Mr Hannibal reeling back from the insult. He rose awkwardly to his feet and boomed into his mobile. "Look, I give everyone my solemn word that if any boar of mine escapes again, I will eat my hat!"

"And a fat lot of good that would do," Mr Golightly retorted, striding past Mr Hannibal without a sideways glance. "I say, BAN them outright!"

"So, listeners," said Sandy Marsh, "if you agree that wild boar farms should be

outlawed, join me and the *Out and About with Sandy Marsh* team at Mr Golightly's protest tomorrow at Hannibals' farm. We'll continue our discussion after this break."

"Who does that man think he is?" huffed Nick.

"Well, I think he has a point," Mum said, fanning herself with a menu. "Those Hannibals *are* useless farmers. All their animals go walkabout. The goats, the blinking peacocks, now the boars…"

"Have any of you ever heard of *Asterix the Gaul*?" asked Sammy, unexpectedly.

Tiger Lily nearly choked on her spaghetti. "The book?"

"Yeah, I got it last Christmas. It wasn't bad … for a book, I mean. At least it's mostly pictures."

SAMMY'S FIRST BOOK REPORT EVER
(as told to Tiger Lily in the Bay Tree Café)

Asterix the Gaul
by Goscinny & Uderzo

Asterix is a Gaul. He has super-human strength when he drinks a magic potion made of mistletoe and stuff. Obelix is his Trusty Companion. Obelix doesn't need the magic potion because he fell into the druid's cauldron when he was a baby. He is so strong that he can carry menhirs - menhirs are huge stones. Their village is the last part of France that is not ruled by the ancient Romans so the Gauls and the Romans are always getting into wicked fights and the Gauls always trick them and win, and afterwards Obelix and Asterix have feasts of WILD BOAR! That's their favourite food.

I give this book: three wild boar

"Actually," said Granny, who had been eavesdropping, "I'd love a regular supply of wild boar. I must have a word with Mrs Hannibal about it." She stroked her chin. "What do you think, Tiger? Perhaps we could even have a wild boar dish of the day?"

So while Mr Hannibal boomed and Mr Golightly whinged on the radio and they marched around the square pretending they couldn't see one another, Sammy drew a menhir on the back page of the menu and Tiger Lily filled it in.

The
Bay
Tree
Café
Wild Boar
Dish of
the Day
Proshutto of
wild boar
with melon
à la romana
Stewed shoulder of
wild boar with
mistletoe roots
à la Obelix
Whole roast striped
boarlet with
Apple Sauce
Wild Boar Sausages
and Gaulish Fries
All dishes served with
a free dose of our
Druid's Magic Potion!
Cheers! Salute!
Cin Cin! Hic!

Tiger was just drawing the cauldron when Mrs Hannibal came into the café. Granny hastily turned off the radio and hissed, "Don't mention the boars."

Then Mr Golightly strode in.

There was an awkward silence and, once again, everyone became very busy stirring and cutting and chewing and fishing under the tables for their napkins.

"Excuse me, ladies and gentlemen," he said, pulling out a notebook. "I'm Julius Golightly of the *Daily Bugle*, as you all know. I'm investigating the local wild boar menace—"

"I PROTEST!" Mrs Hannibal bellowed at him. She marched across the café with her hands on her hips (although her voice was a bit wobbly). "What are you trying to do? Ruin our livelihood?"

Mr Golightly looked down at her from his great height.

96

"As the senior travel writer for the *Daily Bugle*, I have seen a fair share of MEDDLERS and MUDDLERS in every corner of the globe, but I have never come across such bunglers as yourself and your husband…"

He flicked over a page of his notebook. "Are you aware, madam, that you are in violation of Bye-law 4012, subsection 3…"

Granny moved protectively closer to Mrs Hannibal. She knew Electra's bark was worse than her bite.

Spanners Murphy got to his feet. "Steady on, dude," he said. "We don't want any trouble. There are children present…"

"And that's another thing," Mr Golightly continued. "It is absolute lunacy to allow any of these children to set foot on this dog's dinner of a farm." He cast a cold eye on the parents of the K9 Coaching pupils. "No RESPONSIBLE parent would let their children and their dogs within a mile of the place…"

At this, the café erupted.

"…interfering townie…"

"…coming in here…"

"…insulting people…"

"…authorities ought to put a stop to your Dog School at once…"

"Mum, is Mr Golightly trying to shut down K9 Coaching?" Tiger Lily spluttered.

Mum put down her glass and nodded. "I'm sorry, Lily, but he's right in a way. That boar is lethal – just imagine if it attacked one of you. I don't think you should go back. What do you think, Nick?"

Nick raised his shoulders and let them drop. "I think the man is a pompous twit!"

"But what about Rosie?" Lily wailed. "She NEEDS to go to school."

"I'm sorry it's turned out this way, Lily, but we really can't keep that dog. She's crackers. She'll be much better off in a dogs' home."

Tiger Lily's heart flipped over. She had a vision of Rosie, pining away with a broken heart behind the high grey walls of an Institution. "And I will pine away too," she thought, "and *then* Mum will be sorry. And everyone will say, 'If only people had obeyed Lex Tiger Lily'."

Chapter 8

As soon as they were allowed, Tiger Lily, Sammy, Katy and Lauren went outside and climbed into the bay tree. Rosie was dozing underneath with her head on her good front paw. After a while, Streaky Junior came out and crashed about on his skateboard until he twisted his ankle and had to sit down on the bench. Then Danny Malone came out and sat at the opposite end of the bench.

"It's all very well for you lot," Tiger Lily grumbled. "You're all allowed to keep your dogs, but I have a cruel heartless mother

who says Rosie HAS TO GO. So we have to help the Hannibals get rid of the BUG so that K9 Coaching can carry on."

"But we don't like the Hannibals," Katy and Lauren whispered so that Streaky wouldn't hear. After all, Milo Hannibal was his best friend.

"None of us likes the Hannibals, but that doesn't matter. K9 Coaching is Rosie's last chance."

"But," said Sammy, reasonably, "that wild boar IS very WILD! I don't want to be anywhere near it." He was sitting at the end of the branch, aiming his bow and arrow at a peacock that was taking an evening stroll through the square. "And tomorrow morning, there probably won't be a Dog School. Mr Golightly and that radio person are going to be protesting at the farm gate."

"And I just heard your Auntie Pamela saying she would join them," said Streaky Junior. "She said something about towels."

"I don't believe it!" Tiger Lily gasped. "How can she take the BUG's side? He doesn't even like her!"

"My mum and dad are going as well," Danny piped up, "because they don't want boars running around if we have to stay here all month."

"Well, that's funny because *my* dad is protesting about the boars because he doesn't want people asking for their money back," Streaky Junior added.

"And my mum and dad don't want them keeping boars because our house is right opposite their gate," said Katy.

Tiger Lily punched the air. "This means WAR!"

Sammy rolled his eyes. "What are you talking about, Tiger? It's got nothing to do with us."

"Of course it has. Anyone who is on the BUG's side is against Rosie. We must find people who are against the BUG and protest about the protest! That's it – we'll form a protest group."

Sammy froze at the end of his branch. Tiger Lily's eyes were blazing, the way they did when she had one of her Big Ideas. It could only mean trouble.

"Will it be like being in a gang?" asked Lauren. "Can we have passwords and secret codes? Could we have a name?"

"Definitely," said Tiger Lily, "we'll call ourselves the K9 Six."

Katy and Lauren beamed, but Streaky Junior rubbed the tough little black hairs on his upper lip and put on a "too cool to be in a gang" look.

"Our mission," said Tiger excitedly, "is to introduce Lex Tiger Lily."

105

"What's that?" Lauren asked. "Is it in a book?"

"No, it's my new law. **Every** *dog* **has the right to a happy** *dog* **life**. Even the ones that are bonkers. That'll be the K9 Six slogan. In fact, we can have two slogans. The other one is: **Every** *wild boar* **has the right to a happy** *wild boar* **life**."

Streaky Junior suddenly looked interested. "I could spray those somewhere for you, if you like. My dad has loads of paint…"

"NO, NO, HANG ON, Streaky," Sammy jumped out of the tree and pulled Tiger off with him. "Tiger," he hissed, "we'll all be in trouble if Streaky starts writing stuff like that all over the place. Anyway, you can't go to war because of a BOAR."

"I don't see why not. In *Gulliver's Travels*,

106

people went to war about the right way to eat a boiled egg, at the roundy end or the pointy end," Tiger Lily said, airily. "And I'm reading another book where all the fat people and the thin people are mortal enemies. It's called *Fattypuffs and Thinifers*. Have you ever heard of it?"

Tiger Lily's Book Reports
As told to the K9 Six.

Fattypuffs and Thinifers
by André Maurois

Edmund is chubby but his brother Terry is skinny. When they go down a secret staircase in the woods, they end up underground in a very strange world where people are divided into Fattypuffs and Thinifers and have to live in separate lands, so Edmund is sent off to Fattyborough and Terry is sent to Thiniville. The Fattypuffs are jolly and like to eat and drink and have lots of naps; the Thinifers are very fit and work very hard, but tend to be bad-tempered and fly off the handle. Their president is always insulting people saying things like, "You're an IDIOT and a BLOCKHEAD!" just like the BUG. The Fattypuffs and Thinifers hate each other. They go to war over an island that lies between their two countries. Edmund and Terry have to fight on opposite sides until at last they have a Peace Conference and draw up peace terms so that the two countries can be united.

This book is very funny and has fantastic drawings.

I give this book:
five round generals

"So," she continued, "a war to save Rosie and Ermina is PERFECTLY sensible."

She raised one arm above her head and punched the air. "Long live the K9 Six and Lex Tiger Lily. All for one, and one for all."

"Waaargh!" roared Katy and Lauren and Danny.

On the steps of the Old Jam Factory, the peacock turned and looked over its shoulder.

"Waaargh!" it screeched back.

In a flash, Rosie was wide awake and bounding after it.

Chapter 9

SCENE 1

Later that night, the heatwave ended in a spectacular summer storm. The air crackled. Black clouds gathered over the jagged mountains behind The Middle of Nowhere. Rosie whined and shivered until Tiger Lily allowed her to snuggle up beside her in bed. They lay side by side, watching the darkening sky through the skylight window.

Just as they were drifting off to sleep, the

room was lit up by a flash of lightning.

There was a huge clap of thunder. The whole house shook. Books crashed off Tiger Lily's shelves. Rosie howled.

Then, just as the first drops of rain pitter-pattered against the windowpane, there was an even louder clap of thunder and the heavens opened.

Rosie yowled, toppled off the bed and fell down the stepladder into the living room, and then couldn't get up the steps again.

Mum banged the wall.

"Lily! What on earth is going on? Do something about that dog!"

But Rosie didn't stop howling until the thunder stopped. And, in the morning, Lily discovered that she had had a "toilet accident" on the living room rug.

TIGERLILY

SCENE 2

Over at the Hannibals' farm, Mrs Hannibal awoke from a night of troubled dreams, brought on by the heat and the thunder and the torrential rain and the restless mooing and bleating and screeching of cattle and goats and peacocks and the distant barking of a frightened dog. The large mound that was Mr Hannibal gently rose and fell in the bed beside her. Quietly, she slid her feet into her slippers, dragged on her dressing gown and went downstairs, looking forward to a nice cup of tea in the peace and quiet. She shuddered to think of the day ahead with Mr Golightly and his awful protest. They certainly didn't need all this bad publicity. If the farm didn't start making money soon, she and Fergus would have no choice but to sell up and go back to teaching. She winced at the idea.

She had just started to mix up a mash for the peacocks when she became aware of a snuffling sound at the scullery door. Dora, her Dobermann pinscher, heard it too, and gave a low warning growl. But by the time Mrs Hannibal had pulled on her wellies and opened the door, there was nothing there.

Nothing – unless you counted the distinctive footprints that Dora was tracking across the churned up mud of the farmyard.

"Fergus! Milo!" Mrs Hannibal bellowed. "We've had another breakout!"

TIGER LILY

SCENE 3

Back in One-End Street, Tiger Lily had moved from her bed to the sofa in the living room. She was eating a bowl of cereal and writing her K9 Six manifesto with Rosie fast asleep beside her, when Mum swept in, looking terribly cross.

"Lily!" she exclaimed. "Get that dog off the sofa and take her outside!"

Tiger Lily looked at her as if she had just sprouted two red horns.

"But Mum!" she protested. "Pippi Longstocking keeps a HORSE and a MONKEY in her house."

"Don't be silly, Lily!" Mum banged the fridge door shut and sent the Lex Tiger Lily Proclamation flying across the floor. "Pippi Longstocking didn't exist and neither did her horse. You mustn't confuse what you read

114

with what happens in Real Life. Real Life is the muddy paw prints all down the hall. Real Life is a dog that can't climb stairs. Real Life is Pam ringing me to say that that ghastly cyclist – even, if he is right about the boars – is giving her grief about a howling dog keeping him awake. THAT dog, Lily!" She pointed at Rosie, who was still sound asleep. "I'm sorry, but I'm going to look for a greyhound rescue centre. No arguments."

Tiger Lily's eyes blazed. She waved her arm at Rosie with a theatrical flourish. "How could you – how could anyone – reject this poor, defenceless creature just because she has only three legs?" She placed her hand over her heart. "Is she to be taken away from the only home she has ever known, bundled into a van like a criminal and locked up in some horrible dog prison? Is that what you want? Is it?"

Mum let out an exasperated sigh. "Don't be so melodramatic, Lily. It's not the three legs that's the problem. It's the chewing library books and the

116

'toilet accidents' and the chasing and the bolting and the fact that we're out all day…"

Tiger Lily picked up her Proclamation and stuck it back on the fridge door. "I'm sure Astrid Lindgren wouldn't have put Rosie in an Institution where they might put her down."

"Oh Lily!" Mum put her head in her hands. "Nobody is going to put her down. What am I going to do with you?"

Just then, there was a welcome knock at the door. Tiger ran to answer it.

It was Katy and Lauren with their dogs, Mitzi and Snoopy.

Lauren came in chattering. "Tiger, do you know if there is Dog School today? Wow! Have you read all these books? Is that your bed? Can I climb the stepladder? What is that funny smell?"

Mum put down her coffee mug.

"Tiger, why don't you and the girls take your dogs for a walk?" she suggested.

Chapter 10

The BUG's voice was booming through a loudspeaker as Tiger Lily, Lauren and Katy came round the corner of One-End Street.

"It's time to stop these incompetent farmers. Let's ban wild boar farming today!"

"Come on," said Lily, "let's see what's happening."

Mr Golightly and his supporters were already setting up camp outside Hannibals' farm. Tiger Lily was furious to see that Auntie Pamela and Streaky Bacon Senior were helping. They had put out folding chairs and

119

a table and were busy handing out mugs of tea and making placards which Danny's dad, Mr Malone, was tying to the gate.

The BUG was standing on a box, as if he needed to make himself any taller, and shouting into a loudspeaker at a cluster of bystanders that included Sammy, Danny and Streaky Junior.

"Stop this madness, now!" he was yelling. "Dangerous animals like boars have

no place in this, er, peaceful backwater. Sign here if you agree the Hannibals' boar farm must be shut down."

Some of the Highland cows were milling around the corner of the meadow, leaning their shaggy heads over the fence, curiously watching what was going on. After the rain, their long, red coats were steaming as they dried out, giving off a pungent whiff. Mr Golightly sounded as if he was trying to speak without breathing in.

Behind the farm gate, Mr Hannibal sat slumped on his tractor, sunk in the deepest despair. He had locked the gate with a huge padlock and chain, and he too had put up a notice.

The last thing he needed was for anyone to find out that the wretched boar and her boarlets had escaped during the storm and were still on the run. Mrs Hannibal and Dora had gone downriver to look for them, while Milo and Luna had gone upriver. Mr Hannibal's job was to guard the gate and keep everyone off the farm until the boars were recaptured.

Sammy crossed the road when he saw Tiger Lily, Katy and Lauren.

"Dog School's off," he told them. "At least while the protest is on. Mr Hannibal's just told me."

Tiger's face crumpled. "Oh Sammy, what am I going to do? By the time the protest is over and Dog School is back on, it may be too late. Mum is going to send Rosie away."

The four of them turned to look at Rosie, who put on her most mournful expression.

Tiger's heart melted. "Remember the K9 Six slogan, everyone: *Every dog has the right to a happy dog life.* We must fight to the death to save her. Lex Tiger Lily rules!"

Unfortunately, her voice was drowned out by a loud jingle-jangle of tinny music as a large broadcasting van with "Out and About with

Sandy Marsh" written on its side careered around the corner. It splashed to a halt in front of Mr Golightly's camp and out stepped Sandy Marsh with two men carrying cameras and a long microphone with a furry bit at one end. There was a little flutter of applause, led, Tiger Lily was outraged to see, by Auntie Pamela. She gave her a hard stare, but Auntie Pamela just waved and smiled.

After a bit of fussing with his equipment, the soundman gave Sandy the thumbs up and she began to speak.

"This is Sandy Marsh in The Middle of Nowhere. I'm here with the world renowned columnist and travel writer Julius Golightly of the *Daily Bugle* to talk about the dangers of…"

She was just getting into her stride, when the Highland cows suddenly began to bellow. As everyone turned to see what was upsetting them, Ermina and her six boarlets came charging down the meadow between the cows. Ermina flew over the fence in one huge leap, while her boarlets came squealing behind her and squeezed underneath. Sandy Marsh, Mr Golightly and the protestors scattered like field mice as the boars hurtled past, sending the picnic table and mugs flying.

"Come on, K9 Six!" Tiger Lily shouted. "Let's go! Follow that boar!"

Mr Hannibal gave a strangled yelp, jumped off the tractor and, surprisingly nimbly for a man of his age and girth, clambered over the gate and ran after Ermina shouting, "Stop!"

Mr Golightly, Sandy Marsh, the photographer and Auntie Pamela sprinted off after them.

For a moment, the bystanders at the farm gate were too stunned to speak. They just stared at the retreating backsides of Mr Hannibal, the boars, the K9 Six and their dogs. Then they too joined in the chase.

They all galloped along like troops in a battle, over the level crossing and down the hill, with Tiger out in front, and Rosie bounding along as if she was back on the racetrack with the roars of the crowd cheering her on to victory.

At the new road down to the holiday cottages, Ermina suddenly stopped running. She turned to face her pursuers. Her squealing boarlets scattered right, left and centre.

Everyone skidded to a halt.

Ermina stared at them through her small, short-sighted eyes. She was big, very big. She pawed the ground.

Danny and Pugsy turned and legged it; Lauren, Snoopy, Katy and Mitzi (who didn't like walking on wet ground) had already fallen behind, way back.

Of the K9 Six only Tiger Lily, Sammy and Streaky were left. Behind them, Auntie Pamela was screaming operatically.

"Ermina," said Tiger Lily, calmly, in her best Dr *I can talk to the animals* Dolittle voice, "why don't you give yourself up like a good boar and stop causing all this trouble?"

Ermina gave a disgusted snort, did a U-turn and charged away again, crashing over a fence and disappearing towards the river.

Everyone turned to Mr Hannibal to see if he was going to follow her, but Mr Hannibal was bent over, clutching his knees and puffing and wheezing as if he had swallowed a mouth organ. "I seem to have lost my hat," he gasped, "and my knees have given out."

Mr Golightly's face had turned Highland-cattle red. "You're an IDIOT and a DELINQUENT, Hannibal," he roared.

129

That evening, on her radio programme, Sandy Marsh used the term "The Boar War" for the first time.

In the morning, the *Daily Bugle*'s front page had an article by Julius Golightly, thundering about the perils of living in the countryside, and a photograph of the graffiti that "someone" had drawn in swirling letters on the playground wall.

Sky News had picked up the story by the afternoon.

BREAKING NEWS

Seven wild boar are on the loose in The Middle of Nowhere since they escaped from a barn on Hannibals' farm earlier this morning for the third successive day. Police officers and dozens of local volunteers are searching for them.

The police are asking householders and motorists to be vigilant. Sightings should be reported to your nearest police station or by ringing the following number....

Chapter 11

Tiger Lily's Dispatches from the Boar War

Day 9

Ermina and her boarlets have been on the run for nine days. The Middle of Nowhere has become The Centre of the Universe, just like Smoky said. The BUG is still camping at the farm gate, and there are swarms of journalists everywhere so the Boar War is on the news every single day. Sammy's dad says it is because August is the silly season when nothing ever happens so the papers just write mad stories about crop circles and aliens and things like runaway boarlets.

I don't think it's silly. It is not good living in a war zone. Everyone is falling out. Spanners Murphy and Streaky Bacon have had a punch-up. Auntie Pamela has taken the BUG's side and isn't speaking to Granny because she is on Mrs Hannibal's side. Sweetness and Light are spitting nails because Streaky Junior wrote "The Bore is InoSlnt" on their gable wall.

The K9 Six have been protesting about the BUG's protest. We march around the village with placards that say "Save Ermina's bacon" and "Every wild boar has the right to a happy wild boar life" and "Lex Tiger Lily"!

Today we were on the television news at lunchtime, but then Mum's Awful Boss saw me and asked her if she knew "the funny-looking girl from The Middle of Nowhere". She is hopping mad. And then Milo had a row with me and told me to stop my protests because Ermina wasn't having a happy life because she had never lived in the wild even though she is a wild boar.

And worst of all, Mrs Hannibal gave Mum the telephone number of an Institution for Doomed Greyhounds. Even though I was on her side. It is not good. But I will not give up until Lex Tiger Lily becomes law!

That evening, Tiger Lily got an email from the Pied Piper, Auntie Pamela's Polish boyfriend. He had gone back to Krakow for his summer holidays to visit his family.

Tiger read the email again and again.

To:	Tiger Lily
Cc:	
Subject:	War and Peace

Cześć! Tiger

The Middle of Nowhere was on Polish television! Are there really herds of wild boars running through the streets?

I imagine you are loving all the excitement, but the boars would probably prefer a warm bed and a trough of oats! I'm sure if anyone can bring about peace it will be you, Tiger! See you all very soon. Give my love to your mum, Granny and Pamela.

Love and peace

Piotr, the Pied Piper xx

Piotr and Milo were right. Ermina and her babies were not having a happy life. Nobody in The Middle of Nowhere was having a happy life. Everybody had fallen out. Everyone was sick of the sight of Mr Golightly and all the journalists.

Peace. That's what everybody needed. Everybody needed to calm down.

Tiger lay down on her bed and finished reading *Fattypuffs and Thinifers*.

Then she had one of her ingenious ideas. "I will organize a Peace Conference," she told Rosie. "That will bring everyone to their senses, and they will be so grateful when I get rid of the BUG, they will probably want to put up a statue of me in the square. Of me and you."

Chapter 12

The following morning, Tiger Lily hurried down to the farm, bursting to tell everyone her new plan. Mr Hannibal was unlocking the gate to take the tractor out just as she arrived.

He looked a mess. His hair was standing on end and his eyes were red from lack of sleep. Since the breakout, he had spent every night prowling around looking for the elusive Ermina – he was utterly worn out, but, worst of all, he was humiliated. Julius Golightly was writing a daily column called "Hannibal and

the Silence of the Boars". He was the laughing stock of the entire country.

He hurriedly looped the padlock over a gate post and tiptoed back to the tractor, like a man who wished he was invisible. Tiger Lily made her move.

"Mr Hannibal, I have a suggestion," she began, when Sandy Marsh suddenly elbowed her and Rosie out of the way and thrust her microphone in Mr Hannibal's face.

"It's Day 10 here in The Middle of Nowhere and the boars are still on the run. Concerned local holidaymakers say there are hoof marks and broken plants along the river beside the cottages where several young children are staying. Can you comment on that, Mr Hannibal?"

"Well, Sandy," he explained, "it means the boars are still close by, but they must be very stressed by now, trying to find food and shelter. If you'd all go away, I'd be able—"

"I'm sorry, Mr Hannibal," Sandy Marsh interrupted with a giggle, "but I must tell our listeners what's happening here … it really is a picture … three goats have just been chased out of the railway station opposite by the stationmaster. He's waving an umbrella at them and, look out, they're crossing the road now and OOPS, one of them has just overturned Mr Golightly's table and is tucking into one of his posters, the one that

139

says 'Hannibal, keep your word. I've got your hat – now eat it!' Hilarious! And now here comes Mr Golightly. Goodness, Julius, you look cross…"

Mr Golightly looked terrible too. Ten days of campaigning had taken their toll. He was losing his voice. He was weary of the war and the smell of the countryside and Auntie Pamela's opera collection. And recently, he had begun to suspect that his fellow journalists, including Sandy Marsh, were no longer taking his campaign seriously. In a sinister new development, his rival at the *Times* was even suggesting he had released the boars himself just to "hog" the front page of the *Daily Bugle*!

They had even published a photograph of him striding past "The Bore is InoSlnt" graffiti that some buffoon had written on the post office gable. He was becoming a laughing stock.

He stormed up to the gate, pushed Sandy Marsh aside and, towering a full 25cm above Mr Hannibal, croaked, "Get these animals away from me, you incompetent idiot!"

Mr Hannibal jabbed a finger at Mr Golightly's chest. "This is the countryside, you nincompoop, this is where animals live. Why don't you clear off back to where you came from and LEAVE US ALL IN PEACE?"

Tiger Lily seized the moment. She ran to the gate, grabbed the chain, wrapped it around her wrist and the gate post and snapped the padlock shut.

"LONG LIVE PEACE!" she shouted, but no one paid any attention. The goats munched, Mr Golightly and Mr Hannibal fumed and Sandy Marsh giggled.

"Love to the boars!" Tiger roared above the din. "Stop the war now!" Rosie gave a helpful bark. Still no one paid any attention.

Tiger Lily rattled her chains. "Listen up," she pleaded. "I've got this great idea."

At last, one of the photographers noticed her. "Hey, Sandy," he said, "look at the girl with the dog!"

Sandy Marsh turned around. "Be quiet, you blithering idiots!" she snapped at Mr Golightly and Mr Hannibal. "What on earth do you think you are doing, young lady?"

"I'm chaining myself to this gate until everyone stops the war. Ermina is innocent. We need to have a Peace Conference."

"Piffle! I've never heard such an ABSURD and HAREBRAINED idea!" cried Mr Golightly.

"No it isn't," said Tiger, fiercely. "It's all your fault that this village is at war over a boar. Auntie Pamela crosses the road when she sees Granny … Spanners has given Streaky a black eye … and Ermina is too frightened to come home … but especially, it's all your fault that the Dog School is closed and I can't train my dog and so my mum is sending her to an Institution."

She stopped.

Mum had just pulled up in the library van and was storming towards her.

"Lily? What the dickens is going on here? Who has the key to this padlock?" she shrieked. "Who has locked up my daughter? Is this some sort of stunt of yours, Golightly? Mr Hannibal, open this padlock at once."

"Of course, Vicky, of course," Mr Hannibal blustered, patting all his pockets for the key. "Nobody locked her up. It's just a prank. I'll free her right away."

"It's not a prank. I don't want to be free until you all agree to hold a Peace Conference!"

"Give us a smile, Tiger!" shouted one of the photographers.

"Leave her alone," Mum shouted back.

"Why don't you all follow me up to the farmhouse and I'll find the key," Mr Hannibal said, "and we can discuss how to end all this palaver over a cup of tea and a biscuit."

"And leave Lily chained to the gate!!" Mum exploded.

147

"Go to your farmhouse?" Mr Golightly spluttered. "OUT OF THE QUESTION. For the

sake of my honour and the honour of all those who support my campaign, I will not set a foot on your DISGRACEFUL and DISREPUTABLE property."

Mr Hannibal swelled with indignation. "How dare you? You pompous self-important…"

"These are my terms," said Mr Golightly. "And they are not negotiable. If we are to have a Peace Conference, it will be held this evening in Pamela's guest living room."

"OUT OF THE QUESTION!" Mr Hannibal replied, hauling himself up into the tractor seat. "Pamela not only happens to be your landlady, but I have seen her here every day brandishing insolent placards in my face. I bid you all good day."

"STOP!" Tiger Lily shouted, rattling her chains again. She could not believe that her plan was falling apart. "What about my granny's café then?"

"OUT OF THE QUESTION," said Mr Golightly, turning on his heel. "I've seen your granny hobnobbing with Mrs Hannibal."

"What about the Old Jam Factory?"

"OUT OF THE QUESTION!" Mr Hannibal and Mr Golightly said together.

Mr Hannibal started up his tractor. Mr Golightly began to pick up his scattered belongings. One of the goats was munching Mr Hannibal's hat.

"Give me the key!" Mum wailed. "I demand you free my daughter at once."

Tiger Lily rattled her chains to be heard above the din.

"Listen to me! I know a good place that doesn't belong to anyone." She laid a hand on Rosie's head. "All we are saying is give peace a chance. Anyone who has a heart knows that Lex Tiger Lily makes sense."

The photographer and a scrum of press crowded around her.

"Say cheese, Lily!"

"Tell us about this Lex Tiger Lily," Sandy Marsh prompted.

As Lily posed for photos, Mr Hannibal finally found the key in his trouser pocket.

Tiger Lily's Dispatches
from the Boar War

Day 10

Lex Tiger Lily: Every dog has the right to a happy dog life.

It worked! We are going to have a PEACE CONFERENCE tomorrow morning. On the ISLAND! Each side can send a delegation of four representatives. Auntie Pamela, Streaky Bacon Senior and Danny's dad are with Mr Golightly. Opposing them are the Hannibals with Spanners Murphy and Granny Rita. Sandy Marsh is going to be the chairperson and she said that "All Other Interested Parties" can attend as observers, so that means the K9 Six are going. Mum can't because she has her driving test tomorrow. Ermina and the boarlets are still on the loose.

I must go now because I have to write a speech.

Chapter 13

The following morning, Tiger Lily addressed the K9 Six.

"Rosie and I stand before you today on the landing beach of this island and implore you, my loyal K9 Six, to do everything in your power to make this Peace Conference a success. The 'anti-Ermina' protest must end, and Mr Golightly must leave so that Dog School can begin again and this magnificent greyhound, the fastest accelerating animal after the cheetah (well, she would be if she had four legs), a hound with eyesight as keen as a hawk, a hound as handsome as it is lovable, can be trained and live a happy dog life – with me! Lex Tiger Lily must triumph. Stop it, Rosie! Sit! Stay! Heel! Oh for goodness sake, stop it!"

Rosie was acting up. She was tugging and straining at her lead, desperate to break free. Her shoulder muscles rippled. She kept looking at the stand of trees in the middle of the island, and whimpering. Her behaviour was making all the other dogs nervous. X-an and Snoopy and Mitzi and Zog and Pugsy were circling around with their noses to the ground, sniffing the pebbles and the fallen bamboos. They chased each other around the fishing hut, barking and yelping, until Tiger Lily called everyone to attention.

"K9 Six, hold on to your leads. Here come the delegations."

Mr Golightly, Pamela and Danny's dad

153

were the first to appear. They marched over the bridge in single file and down to the riverbank. Streaky Bacon Senior came panting behind them, lost his footing on the first stone, toppled off and paddled the rest of the way.

The Hannibals arrived from the other bank. They screeched across the fields in their jeep, sped through the river and drove on to the island, sending up sprays of gravel and water. Spanners Murphy, Granny Rita

and Milo were hanging on for dear life in the back seat.

Next came Sandy Marsh, jumping elegantly over the stepping stones in her flowery wellingtons.

After that came a jolly chattering procession led by Nick the Chippie, Sweetness and Light and a motley collection of Other Interested Parties, many of whom had brought rugs and folding picnic chairs.

All this time, Rosie was going berserk, tugging at her lead, bouncing up at Tiger Lily and looking over her shoulder at the distant clump of oak trees.

Sandy Marsh stepped forward. "It is a great honour to open this historic…"

"One moment please," Mr Golightly held up a long finger. "Before we begin, I wish to register my annoyance that the Hannibal delegation have brought their own seating." He pointed at their jeep. "And furthermore, it appears they intend to stuff their faces…"

(It was true that Granny Rita had a large food hamper on her lap.)

"…while we," Mr Golightly's voice rose, "have neither seating nor refreshments… If this situation is not remedied within ten minutes, I shall have no alternative but to instruct my delegation to follow me off the island. This is an ultimatum."

156

The Other Interested Parties booed and cheered. Tiger Lily's heart sank. The man was an IDIOT and a DUNDERHEAD. Distracted, she let Rosie's lead slip off her wrist.

Rosie didn't hesitate. She was off like the wind.

"ROSIE, NO!" Tiger Lily roared, sprinting after her. "COME BACK. HEEL."

But Rosie paid no attention. She bounded towards the distant clump of oak trees, from which there now came an excited outbreak of grunting and squealing.

The two delegations looked at each other. Mrs Hannibal was out of the jeep in an instant with Dora.

"It's Ermina and the boarlets. That greyhound has seen her. Bravo, Rosie! Milo, Dora, Luna, follow that greyhound!"

Rosie, the second fastest accelerating land animal after the cheetah, tore ahead of all the others. She was magnificent. And Lily, with all the energy and grace of a tiger, sprinted after her.

Side-stepping, jigging, bouncing and leaping, they chased the first boarlet out of the undergrowth to the whistles, shouts, yells and howls of the delegations, the chairperson and the Other Interested Parties.

158

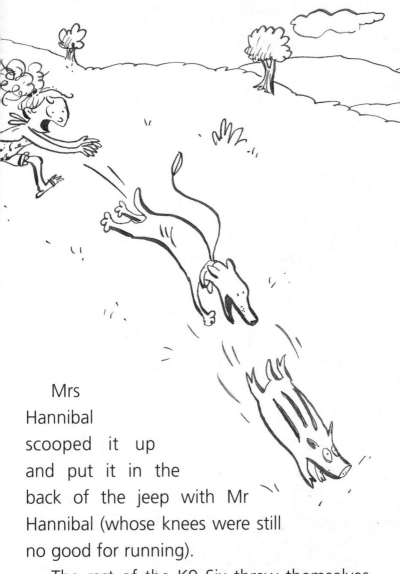

Mrs
Hannibal
scooped it up
and put it in the
back of the jeep with Mr
Hannibal (whose knees were still
no good for running).

The rest of the K9 Six threw themselves
enthusiastically into the chase.

Snoopy and Zog, like the good hunting breeds they were, howled to let Katy and Sammy know when they had sniffed out more boarlets, rounded them up and flushed them out of the woods. Streaky Junior and his German shepherd then took over, shepherding them towards the jeep, with X-an gently nipping the boarlets' ears to keep them all together.

Danny and Pugsy played their part by keeping up a steady flow of yaps.

At the last minute, one of the captured boarlets scrambled out of the jeep and made a run for the river.

160

"Go for it, Mitzi," shouted Mrs Hannibal and Mitzi splashed happily off into the water, as if

remembering her ancestral hunting life as a German Pudel hauling wildfowl out of the marshes. She grabbed it by the scruff of its neck and safely brought it back to shore, where Mrs Hannibal was waiting to scoop it up and pop it back with its sisters. "I told you poodles love water," she told Katy.

Then Ermina came out of cover with Milo and Luna, his bloodhound, behind her.

"Form a cordon, everybody," Mrs Hannibal barked. "Line up opposite one another."

Spanners and Streaky, Smoky and Milo, Granny Rita, Pamela, Nick the Chippie, Sweetness and Light, the K9 Six and Other Interested Parties hastily ran to form two lines opposite one another, while Milo and Luna herded Ermina down to the shore.

"Drive her towards the hut, Milo," shouted Tiger Lily. "Sammy, open the door."

And Ermina, proud as a bride on the way to her wedding, trotted amiably through the excited line of her best friends and neighbours, and ran into the hut.

Sammy banged the door shut.

"Reward your dogs!" Mrs Hannibal barked. "Well done, the K9 Six! Well done, everyone."

Granny and Auntie Pamela were holding on to each other and crying with relief. Streaky and Spanners were giving each other high fives and Danny's tiny dad and tall Mr Golightly and stout Mr Hannibal were in a group hug.

"Is it all over, Tiger?" Lauren piped up. "Do we get a prize? Will your mum let you keep Rosie now?"

Then there was an almighty crash of thunder and the heavens opened.

"Come on, everyone," shouted Granny Rita. "Follow me."

Tiger Lily's Dispatches
from the Boar War
Day 11 16:30

Lex Tiger Lily: Every dog has the right to a happy dog life.

Today has been the most exciting day of my life! The Boar War is over and the K9 Six are heroes. We captured the boarlets, and all because of clever Rosie with the good eyes and the fast legs. Mrs Hannibal says she is EXCEPTIONAL.

Once the boars were recaptured, Streaky Bacon took Ermina back to Hannibals' farm in his van and Mr Hannibal took the boarlets in the jeep. Then Granny Rita invited everyone to the Bay Tree Café to hold the Peace Conference out of the rain and, for once, the BUG didn't argue.

"Ladies and gentlemen," he said in his Act of Surrender, "I am leaving on the next train. You and your rampaging boars, your

wandering goats and screeching peacocks, your assorted hounds, illiterate wall scribblers and gangs of wild children may henceforth hurtle and career freely around The Middle of Nowhere and sink into the obscurity you so rightly deserve. You are yesterday's news. The story is moving on and Julius Golightly must fearlessly move with it."

Surprisingly, nobody took offence. Indeed, Pamela offered to help him pack. Granny made him up a packed lunch, Mrs Hannibal gave him a present of a hand-knitted angora scarf and Spanners carried his case to the station. I got the K9 Six to give him a guard of honour as he boarded the 13:15, and Smoky Bacon gave him a free timetable. He left his bike and his helmet behind, saying he would never ride a bike again. I asked if I could have the helmet.

Then we all ran back to the café to get out of the rain, and Mum was there, all glowy and excited because she had passed her driving test.

"And the best thing is, now I can drive around the mountains in my lovely new library van and I won't have to work in the City with my Awful Boss."

And everybody, the two delegations and the Other Interested Parties clapped and gave her high fives and Sammy did a drum roll on the counter and even Sweetness and Light cheered.

And that's when I had an IDEA. I would make a Peace Plan so that every single person in The Middle of Nowhere, not just Ermina and Rosie, could have a happy life and never go to war again.

Chapter 14

It was nearly seven o'clock when Mum and Tiger Lily went home to One-End Street. Mum sat on the sofa and read the papers. Rosie lay exhausted on the rug with her legs in the air. Tiger Lily was upstairs on her bed, doing something with the peacock feathers.

"This was never about saving Ermina and her boarlets, was it, Lily?" Mum said, after a bit.

"No, Mum. It was about saving Rosie. You mustn't send her away. I love her."

At the mention of her name, Rosie

opened her eyes and stood up. Mum looked at Rosie's long face. Rosie looked at Mum with her big, brown, gentle eyes. "Mrs Hannibal says that greyhounds make brilliant pets," Tiger Lily said, as casually as she could. "Especially when they know who's the leader of the pack."

Mum folded up her newspaper.

"And she says greyhounds don't shed hairs so even if Rosie sometimes *accidentally* sits on the sofa, your clothes won't get hairy."

Mum looked at Rosie.

Rosie looked at Mum.

"And they have no sweat glands so they don't smell…" She paused for a second, but when Mum didn't say anything she carried on. "The ancient Egyptians worshipped them, you know."

Mum let out a long sigh. "But, Tiger, what would we do when you're at school and I'm at work?"

Tiger Lily's heart skipped a beat. "Well," she said, "I've been thinking about that." She climbed down her ladder and cleared a space on the sofa. "Mrs Hannibal says that Rosie was probably used to travelling all over the country when she was a racing greyhound so you could take her to work with you in your lovely new library lorry. And she'd be really good and gentle and all the old ladies would love her and the old men would pretend to remember her as a racer and all the children would come to borrow books so that they could see her so, you see, she would be helping you…"

171

"DON'T BE SILLY, LILY! My Awful Boss would have a fit."

"Your Awful Boss mightn't have to know." Tiger Lily laid her head on Mum's shoulder. Rosie laid her head on Mum's knee and gazed at her with her far-sighted eyes. Mum looked at the Proclamation of Lex Tiger Lily on the fridge door.

"Well maybe, for a trial period…"

"Oh Mum, I love you!"

Outside in the garden a peacock screeched. Tiger Lily jumped to her feet. "I nearly forgot! Sammy's going back to his mum today. I've made him a present. I'll need my sword. And Piotr's arriving. Auntie Pamela told me. Come on!"

Tigerlily

They were just in time. Sammy and his dad were already on the station platform.

"I have a reward for you," Lily said, setting down a bulging carrier bag at Sammy's feet, "but you have to kneel down first."

Sammy looked around to see who was watching, but there was nobody but his dad and Tiger's mum. "I'm not marrying you," he said adamantly. "No way."

Tiger Lily gave an exasperated sigh. "I don't want you to marry me. Kneel down."

Sammy knelt down. Tiger Lily drew the wooden sword from her belt and struck Sammy on the shoulder. "I now proclaim thee, my Trusty Companion, Governor of Oak-tree Island, Keeper of the Hut Door, Baron Sammy of the Order of the Wild Boar and Lord of the Peacock."

She grinned. "You may now arise and take your reward."

Sammy gingerly peered into the bag. "What?!" His face was a picture of confusion and disappointment. It was Mr Golightly's abandoned cycling helmet, decorated with the three peacock feathers.

"Isn't it fabulous?" Tiger Lily beamed. "It's a real Governor's hat with a plume of feathers! You said you wanted a high-hat."

"Tiger," said the new Governor of Oak-tree Island, Keeper of the Hut Door, Baron Sammy of the Order of the Wild Boar and Lord of the Peacock, "that's not a hi-hat. A hi-hat is a sort of cymbal."

Tiger Lily looked blank.

"It's a musical instrument."

Lily shrugged. "Never heard of it."

"Part of a drum kit. Two cymbals on a stand with a foot pedal."

"Oh!" She turned a little red. "You could still wear it on the island…"

"No," said Sammy. "No. I'm not putting it on. Not ever. I'm not."

"Oh, go on," said Nick, "and I'll take a photo of you both." And he did, just as the train pulled into the station, with everyone looking out of the windows.

LILY'S PEACE PLAN

IT IS DECREED:

* That Mum will make a website for the Hannibals so that they can sell their Highland beef and wild boar and don't lose the farm.

* That Spanners Murphy and Nick the Chippie will help repair the fencing on Hannibals' farm.

* That the K9 Six will clean the graffiti off the station, the post office and the swings.

* That Granny Rita and Mrs Hannibal will run cookery weekends, so that the people who come can stay at Auntie Pamela's B&B or Streaky Bacon's cottages.

* That as a thank you to Tiger Lily for this excellent Road Map for Peace, which will bring peace, prosperity and goodwill to all, her law, Lex Tiger Lily, will be adopted throughout The Middle of Nowhere SO THAT...

* Mrs Hannibal can start Dog School again and train Rosie without further delay.
MISSION ACCOMPLISHED!

The Beautiful
PLANTS
of
SEYCHELLES

Adrian and Judith Skerrett

Camerapix Publishers International
NAIROBI

First published 1991 by
Camerapix Publishers International,
P. O. Box 45048,
Nairobi,
Kenya

© Camerapix 1991

ISBN 1 874041 05 9

This book was designed and produced by
Camerapix Publishers International

Edited by Brian Tetley
Production Editor: Debbie Gaiger
Design: Kimberly Davis

Printed in Hong Kong.

*Page 1: Sprays of spectacular Bougainvillea grace every Seychelles garden. Previous pages: Tall
African Tulip Trees offer their orange cups to the sun. Below: The yellow variety of Peacock
Flower; multi-coloured Portulaca; the fiery Hibiscus flower, symbol of the tropics; and the
speckled Canna Lily. Following pages: Scarlet clusters of flowers of the aptly named Flame Tree.*

Contents

Preface

With more than 1,100 species of plant to choose from, of which 250 or so occur naturally and about seventy-five are found nowhere else on earth, this book is a mixture of the most colourful, the most interesting, the most bizarre, the most common wildflowers, the most popular garden plants, the rarest and most exotic of Seychelles flora and tropical plants.

It is hoped it will help you identify and appreciate some of the fascinating and attractive plants found in the gardens and on the roadsides, beaches, and mountains of Seychelles. Some thrive in the hot, humid lowlands, others prefer the cooler hills, while a few enjoy the salt air and exploit shoreline niches.

Seychelles has plants so unique — and so rare — that in natural conditions they can be seen on only a few hilltops of Mahé or on just on one small island. Among them are the Jellyfish Plant (*Medusagyne oppositifolia*) and Wright's Gardenia (*Rothmannia annae*). Such is the range of habitats the islands offer that around each corner lies something of interest for the plant-watcher.

Though not so marked as those in Europe, the seasons bring their own, more subtle changes. During the dry, South-East Monsoon, the Bougainvillea (*Bougainvillea glabra*) is at its most spectacular, while Napoleon (*Flemingia strobilifera*) and Candle Bush (*Caesalpinia alata*) bloom in the lowlands — and for a few weeks, the telegraph wires are festooned with misty-white sprays of Bridal Bouquet (*Porana paniculata*). In October and November, just as the first rains arrive, the glorious Flame Trees (*Delonix regia*) burst into blazing beauty, and the fat buds on the Crinum Lilies open out to reveal a more serene loveliness.

Whenever you visit Seychelles, something will catch your eye to delight and intrigue you. We hope that this book answers many questions about these natural treasures of Seychelles.

Introduction

The Seychelles Islands are one of the most beautiful places on earth, fortunate to escape the massive deforestation which so many of her sister Indian Ocean islands have suffered.

Indispensible to this beauty is the rich greenery which swathes most islands, setting the turquoise sea and silver beaches in exquisite relief against a deep emerald backdrop of forest and garden.

When men first saw Seychelles they spoke, as many still do, of 'an Earthly Paradise'. General Gordon, later to die in defence of Khartoum, spent some gentler times in Seychelles, and became convinced they were the very Garden of Eden. The fascinating Coco de Mer was his Tree of Knowledge.

What you see now looks much the same as the sights which greeted the first British visitors in 1609, but many of the species found growing in the valleys and clinging to the ridges are different today.

French colonists exulted at finding magnificent timber trees, hardwoods of a type never seen before, eighty feet high and sixteen feet in circumference, which were perfect for ship building.

Though few in number, some of these endemics, evolved over centuries of isolation in undisturbed forests, still survive. But many former giants — *bwa d fer* (*Vateria seychellarum*), *bwa d nat* (*Mimusops seychellarum*), and *bwa d montanny* (*Campnosperma seychellarum*) — are today weak, stunted specimens, as though man's onslaught had robbed them of their pride. Nevertheless, they kindle the imagination and cause many to think of how it must have been.

Yet the delicate Jellyfish Tree, perhaps rare even in the seventeenth century, still clings to survival on the abyss of extinction in its mountain strongholds.

Many of these endemics began to pursue a separate evolutionary path long before the mammals evolved. Some are

hard to see and disappointing to the non-specialist eye, but others, such as the Coco de Mer (*Lodoicea maldivica*) and the Pitcher Plant (*Nepethnes pervillei*) challenge the imagination with their form and life histories, while Wright's Gardenia and Vanilla Orchid (*Vanilla phalaenopsis*) display a beauty that would grace any florist's window.

The second layer of Seychelles' flora consists of those plants and trees which made their own way there and flourished. Some clung to the feathers of migratory birds or were washed ashore by the sea thousands of years ago to become very much a part of the natural scene.

Finally, and often most noticeably, there are the plants which man brought there to exploit or for aesthetic reasons. Seychelles has a climate in which these showy exotics thrive, and no visitor can fail to admire their abundant beauty. The popular pan-tropicals fill gardens with colour, or provide medicines, dyes, timber, fibre, fruits, and spices.

You find something growing in every available location. In the dry, sandy soil of the beachheads unlikely Spider Lilies (*Hymenocallis littoralis*) thrive and great Takamaka trees (*Calophyllum inophyllum*) lean over to offer kindly shade from the midday sun.

Amid the dappled light of the coconut plantations, in a tangle of fallen palm leaves and mounds of coconut husks, grow cheerful *kokets* (*Turnera ulmifolia*) and sapphire-blue spikes of *zepi ble* (*Stachytarpheta urticifolia*). And everywhere there is the fragrance and the beauty of the hibiscus, bougainvillea, and frangipani.

As the land rises, the air becomes cooler and the vegetation changes. Where the cloud clings to the peaks, great forest trees flourish and the mist forest with its own unique flora, twisted

and gnarled, predominates. Every branch is thickly padded with vivid green mosses, and every hollow occupied by some unique orchid or plumes of ferns.

On the coral islands, plants have adapted to survive the onslaught of salt-laden spray. The fringes of the beaches are lined with hardy shrubs and trees, such as Cordia (*Cordia subcordata*), Sea Hibiscus (*Hibiscus tiliaceus*), and Fish Poison Tree (*Barringtonia asiatica*).

The Seychelles Islands are vibrant with life, colour, beauty and spectacle — thanks in no small measure to their rich floral heritage. There is plant life everywhere — on the wildest coast, the hottest sheet of granite glacis, the deepest mountain crevasse.

Left: The Coco de Mer palm. Top: Sweet-scented flowers grow on long catkins of the male tree. Above: The large, double coconut of the female tree.

1. PALMS AND PANDANUS

COCO DE MER (Koko-d-mer)
Lodoicea maldivica

In its natural state, the Coco de Mer is confined to Praslin and Curieuse. It was reported to have also occurred on three small islands near Praslin: Round, Chauve Souris, and St. Pierre.

There are separate male and female trees, the latter bearing the famous double coconut, the world's largest seed. The male tree has an enormous catkin covered in many tiny, yellow, sweet-scented, starlike flowers.

Before the discovery of Seychelles the Coco de Mer was known only from a few nuts washed ashore in the Maldives, said to have been from trees which grew under the sea. Because of their erotic form and rarity, huge sums were paid for them. However, since the nuts soon become waterlogged in sea water it may be that Seychelles was known to Arab traders who guarded their secret jealously.

The female does not bear nuts until it is twenty-five years old, and takes perhaps 200 years to reach full size. Young nuts contain a delicately flavoured jelly sometimes served as a dessert. Mature nuts may be sold whole, turned into fruit bowls, or used as balers for fishing boats.

General Gordon, of Khartoum fame, developed the theory that Praslin's Vallée de Mai, home of the Coco de Mer, was the site of the Garden of Eden, while the tree was the forbidden fruit.

COCONUT PALM (Koko)
Cocos nucifera

It is not known whether the coconut palm is indigenous to Seychelles or if it was brought there by Polynesians, Arabs, or other ocean explorers before the first Europeans. Whatever the truth, today the swaying coconut palm is a feature of every Seychelles beach.

The flesh of the nut is eaten raw, or dried and crushed to extract coconut oil. Copra, dried coconut flesh, was once the major export of Seychelles. Coconut cream is extracted by pouring warm water over the grated flesh. After about an hour the juice is squeezed out and allowed to stand, the cream being skimmed from the top of the liquid. Coconut cream is used to flavour Seychelles curries, and as a topping for fruit salads.

The fibre of the husk can be used to make ropes and door mats. It is also a popular fuel for barbecues. The leaves are used for thatching, weaving, and fish traps.

Illustrated on following page

SEYCHELLES PANDANUS (Vakwa maron)
Pandanus seychellarum

Pandanus or Screwpines are tropical trees with stilt roots and spiral rosettes of leaves. Eight species are found in Seychelles, of which five are unique to the islands.

Most impressive of all is the Seychelles Pandanus, a medium-sized tree with spectacular stilt roots growing directly from high on the trunk. It bears a stalked, pineapple-like fruit about thirty centimetres (one foot) wide. It often grows on inaccessible clifftops, sending roots deep down into the river valleys.

Illustrated on previous page

BALFOUR'S PANDANUS (Vakwa rivyer)
Pandanus balfourii

Also unique to Seychelles, Balfour's Pandanus is common along the coast of all the main granitic islands. It is a slender tree bearing a spiral mass of drooping leaves and medium-sized fruits.

Illustrated on following page

CA
Co

Th
wo
ca
dia
fou

wl
us

FIS
Ba

A
lea
fou
ha
giv

fib
tra
ne

wl
un

Fo

FLAME TREE (Flambwayan)
Delonix regia

Also known as Royal Poinciana, Peacock Flower, Flamboyant, and Fancy Anna, this is one of the world's most magnificent trees. Originating from Madagascar, it is a common ornamental lowland tree on all the main islands.

Around the end of the year, it blooms like a scarlet umbrella with clusters of bright red flowers with five petals, one of which is usually white or yellow. Its long brown pods, sixty centimetres (two feet) in length, take two years to ripen.

The Flame Tree is practically extinct in its native home due to forest clearance. In Madagascar it was only rediscovered as recently as 1828, in a location where it had probably been planted by Arab traders, and it was not found in a truly wild state until 1932.

Illustrated on previous page

FRANGIPANI (Franzipann)
Plumeria obtusa

A small cultivated tree with dark rhododendron-like leaves and clusters of large, white, fragrant flowers. The arrangement of the petals resembles a fan or propeller.

Originating from the West Indies, it is often planted near temples and cemeteries in India and South-East Asia. The name probably derives from the French 'frangipanier', meaning coagulated milk, a reference to the white, poisonous juice that exudes from the stem.

A red variety, (*Plumeria rubra*) from Central America, is also common in Seychelles. The slightly fleshy, fragrant flowers may be red, pink, yellow, or a combination of colours.

Illustrated on following page

GEIGER TREE (Pors)
Cordia sebestena

This medium-sized tree is a popular ornamental in the streets of Victoria and hotel gardens. Also known as the Geranium Tree, it was introduced to Seychelles from the Caribbean.

It has large oval leaves up to twenty-five centimetres (ten inches) and clusters of orange flowers four centimetres (1.5 inches) long. Small, pear-shaped, white fruits develop.

PORCHER (Pors)
Cordia subcordata

This related tree grows on the coast to a height of nine metres (thirty feet) and has oval leaves twenty-five centimetres (ten inches) long. The flowers are a paler orange than those of the Geiger Tree, but similar in shape, up to four centimetres (one and a half inches) wide. The white fruits are like those of the Geiger Tree, but turn black as they mature.

The *Cordia* genus is named after two German botanists, Enricius and Valerius Cordus, father and son, while the local name Porcher is a corruption of the Tamil word 'puarassu'. The Creole name, 'pors', is the same for both trees, the two species not being distinguished. The tree is native to a wide area, ranging from East Africa to Polynesia.

Previous page: Top: Geiger Tree, Bottom: Porcher

JELLYFISH TREE (Bwa mediz)
Medusagyne oppositifolia

Distantly related to tea but in a family of its own, this strange tree is found only on three Mahé hilltops. Unseen since 1908, its rediscovery in June 1970 caused a botanic sensation.

An ancient and primitive tree, it grows up to nine metres (thirty feet), with spreading branches. Small, white, many-stamened flowers develop into brown umbrella-like fruits, said to resemble jellyfish. The fruits contain minute, flat, winged seeds. Attempts to propagate the tree from seedlings have been largely unsuccessful and it remains one of the rarest plants in the world — perhaps only thirty specimens exist.

Illustrated on following page

MANGROVE (Manglye)

A dense belt of mangroves once swathed much of the coast of Mahé. Port Glaud, Anse Boileau, and Mont Fleuri have remnants of these once extensive coastal swamps. Many other larger islands also retain mangroves. They grow between high and low water, generally near river mouths.

Some have aerial roots called pneumatophores which help with respiration. One of the most common is the Red Mangrove (*Rhizophora mucronata*), with distinctive arched stilt roots, adapted to survival furthest from land. Seeds germinate on the tree and drop when they have a shoot about fifty centimetres (twenty inches) long. If it is low tide they stick in the mud and put out stilt roots.

By contrast, the Puzzlenut or Manglye ponm (*Xylocarpus granatum*) grows close to muddy shores. It develops a spherical fruit fifteen centimetres (six inches) in diameter, containing many irregular-shaped seeds which fit together like a jigsaw puzzle to give it its English name. It is also called Chinese Puzzle and Manglye pasyanas (Patience Mangrove) due to this unusual feature.

Illustrated on previous page

ORCHID TREE (Sabo bef)
Bauhinia variegata

A small ornamental tree with year-round pink or mauve, orchid-like flowers, five centimetres (two inches) across, and bi-lobed leaves shaped like a cow's hoof print. The seed pods are sixty centimetres (two feet) long. The tree, which originated in tropical America, is also known as Bull-hoof, Mountain Ebony, Poor Man's Orchid, and Napoleon's Hat. There are showier, cultivated varieties.

Illustrated on following page

TRAVELLER'S TREE (Bannann voyaz)
Ravenala madagascariensis

This ornamental tree-like plant is related to the banana. It has a fan-shaped arrangement of banner-like leaves, and a stout spike of white bracts and flowers. The leaves have long pale stalks emerging from a palm-like trunk. It is a native of Madagascar.

A traveller can always find a drink by breaking off a leaf stalk, which can hold up to two litres (three pints) of liquid. The bright blue seeds produce a pleasantly scented antiseptic oil, and the trunk a sugary sap.

Illustrated on previous page

YELLOW FLAME (Flam zon)
Peltophorum pterocarpum

Yellow Flame is a large, ornamental tree, with feathery leaves and dramatic erect stems of bright yellow flowers. The pods are rusty brown. It originates from Malaysia, where a brown dye used for batiks is extracted from its light grey bark.

Illustrated on following page

3. SHRUBS

ALLAMANDA (Alamanda zonn)
Allamanda cathartica

A common ornamental and escaping shrub, its other names include Large Yellow Bells, Golden Trumpet, and Heavenly Chief due to the conspicuous golden yellow funnel-shaped flowers eight centimetres (three inches) across.

The genus is named after the Dutch botanist Allamand, while *cathartica* refers to its use as a purgative. The plant also contains a poisonous latex. It originates from Brazil.

Another species, Mauve Allamanda (*Allamanda violacea*) is also common. Apart from its mauve-pink flowers, it is similar in appearance to the yellow form.

Illustrated on previous page

BOUGAINVILLEA (Vilea)
Bougainvillea sp.

The long, vibrantly colourful sprays of this symbol of the tropics actually consist of bracts, the flowers being small, white and tubular in shape. The plant forms hedges which often completely cover walls or granite boulders.

The most commonly seen is purple, (*Bougainvillea glabra*), but there are many varieties of *Bougainvillea spectabilis* including pink, orange, white, yellow, red, with various shades of colour in between. A hybrid variety bears purple and white bracts on the same stem. The woody stem is covered in thorns.

It originates from Brazil and is named after the French navigator Louis de Bougainville. It flowers all year-round, but is most spectacular during the drier South-East Monsoon.

Illustrated on following page

CANDLE BUSH (Katepan)
Cassia alata

A small shrub up to two metres (seven feet) high with spikes of yellow flowers. Its winged pods, which turn from green to black, contain triangular seeds.

Other names include Seven Golden Candlesticks, God's Candle, Roman Candle, Ringworm Plant, and Golden Bush. It originates from tropical America.

The leaves contain chrysophanic acid, a fungicide used to treat fungal skin infections. The seeds are a purgative and a vermifuge for deworming. The bark is used in tanning. It flowers only during the dry months of the South-East Monsoon.

Illustrated on previous page

GIANT MILKWEED
Calotropis gigantea

Also known as Mader, and Yercum, this plant is a relatively recent arrival in Seychelles but a successful coloniser because of its ability to survive in poor soils and resistance to salt spray.

Its stout woody stem grows to four metres (thirteen feet) high, bearing fleshy leaves covered in stiff white hairs. The mauve, star-shaped flowers grow in clusters at the end of its branches.

It originates from India and South-East Asia, where it is used for rope making, fishing lines, and nets due to the high quality of its stem fibre known as Yercum. The milky latex is used to remove hairs from hides, and for medicinal purposes. The large inflated fruits contain 'vegetable silk' which serves as a stuffing material, similar to kapok.

Illustrated on following page

CORAL HIBISCUS (Ibiskis koray)
Hibiscus schizopetalus

This East African variety of Hibiscus is notable for its frilly petals and long, hanging stamen. Other names include Fringed Hibiscus and Chinese Lantern.

TURK'S CAP
Malvaviscus arboreous

Looking like a closed Red Hibiscus, or Turk's fez, this shrub is also known as Sleeping Hibiscus, Pepper Hibiscus, Cardinal's Hat, and Wax Mallow.

Previous page: Top: Coral Hibiscus, Bottom: Turk's Cap

LILAC MORNING GLORY
Ipomoea carnea

Common in coastal areas, this shrub has triangular leaves ten centimetres (four inches) long, and showy clusters of lilac pink, funnel-shaped flowers up to ten centimetres (four inches) wide. It originates from tropical America.

Illustrated on following page

NAPOLEON
Flemingia strobilifera

This shrubby plant, up to one and a half metres (five feet) in height, has heart-shaped leaves and long flowering stems consisting of light brown bracts enclosing small purple flowers. The shape of the bract is said to resemble Napoleon's hat.

It is a common plant, especially in the lowlands of Mahé, Praslin, and La Digue. It originates from South-East Asia. The genus is named after John Flemming, an early nineteenth-century British botanist.

Illustrated on previous page

OLEANDER (Laryer ros)
Nerium oleander

A tall, ornamental shrub, up to four metres (thirteen feet), with stiff pointed leaves about twenty centimetres (eight inches) long in groups of three. It bears pink, double flowers — sometimes single — varying in colour from red to white.

Other names include Rose Bay. It occurs from the Mediterranean to Asia. The plant is extremely poisonous. People have died from eating meat cooked on oleander skewers including, on one occasion, some soldiers of Alexander the Great.

YELLOW OLEANDER (Laryer zonn)
Thevetia peruviana

This closely related species from Central and South America is also known as Be Still and Lucky Nut. The leaves are narrower and shiny on the upper side, and the flowers are yellow and tubular. The fruit contains two large, flat seeds, often worn as jewellery or carried in the pocket to bring good luck.

In its milky juice, the plant contains the cardiac glucoside, *thevetin*, a poison that causes vomiting, convulsions, and weakness of the pulse. A heart drug is produced from the fruit.

Amongst Hindus, Yellow Oleander is often chosen as an offering to the god Shiva. An orange-coloured form also exists.

Illustrated on following page

PEACOCK FLOWER (Zegret)
Caesalpinia pulcherrima

An ornamental, pyramid-shaped shrub also known as Pride of Barbados, Dwarf Poinciana, Mexican Bird of Paradise, and Flamboyant, it bears bright clusters of fiery orange flowers with long, projecting stamens, at the tips of its branches. It has a lacy foliage and flowers all year-round.

Believed to originate from South America, it is now unknown there in its wild state. Besides the usual orange form, there are yellow and red varieties. Young seeds are eaten raw. The flowers and leaves are used to reduce fever and the leaves as a purgative.

The sweet-scented flowers yield a good quality honey and tannin is obtained from the fruits.

Illustrated on previous page

RED HOT CATS' TAILS (Ke-d-mimi)
Acalypha hispida

This is a garden ornamental from the West Indies, also known as Chenille Plant, Monkey Tail, or Pussy Tail. It is a medium-sized shrub with heart-shaped leaves twenty centimetres (eight inches) long and drooping, furry, dark red catkins forty-five centimetres (eighteen inches) long.

The tails are made up of staminate flowers without petals. The leaves may be cooked and eaten. It is often used medicinally.

WRIGHT'S GARDENIA (Bwa sitron)
Rothmannia annae

In its natural state, this beautiful shrub occurs only on Aride Island. It grows up to four metres (thirteen feet) in height. Solitary, trumpet-shaped white flowers with magenta spots appear about ten days after heavy rain. They have a fragrant smell, and are one of the most beautiful of Seychelles' endemic flowers. The fruits are green, shiny and lemon-shaped.

It is thought Wright's Gardenia used to occur on the hills of Mahé, Praslin, and Félicitè but disappeared, possibly due to soil erosion.

Illustrated on following page

4. CLIMBERS

BEACH MORNING GLORY (Patatran)
Ipomoea pes-caprae

Also known as Sea Morning Glory, this climber trails over granite boulders by the sea and along the seashore on all islands. The creeping root stems reach up to ten metres (thirty-three feet) or more in length. It bears purple-pink, trumpet-shaped flowers and circular leaves with a notch at the tip, reminiscent of a goat's hoof print.

The plant is pan-tropical. The seeds germinate and grow in sea water which has contributed to its success. It is used as a purgative and for other medicinal purposes.

RAILWAY CREEPER
Ipomoea cairica

This is a related creeper, common along roadsides from sea level to middle altitudes. It has deeply divided leaves like the fingers of a hand. The mauve, bell-shaped flowers wither by mid-morning.

The plant originates from Africa, but its name derives from India, where it spread rapidly along railway lines.

Previous page. Top: Beach Morning Glory. Bottom: Railway Creeper

CORAL CREEPER (Antigonn)
Antigonon leptopus

Common along roadsides and open areas, this climbing plant grows on fences and over shrubs. Clusters of bright pink flower sprays end in tendrils. Each flower is made up of five sepals and no petals. The leaves are heart-shaped with wavy edges. A white form also exists.

Originating from Mexico, other names include Mexican Creeper, Coral Vine, Bride's Tears, Pink Vine, Queen's Wreath, and Queen's Jewels.

Illustrated on following page

PASSION FLOWER (Granadilla)
Passiflora edulis

This vine bears flowers up to ten centimetres (four inches) wide, with white petals, and a purple and white centre of many filaments, that opens in the afternoon. The round, green fruit becomes purple when ripe or, in the variety, *flavicarpa*, yellow.

The distinctive flower is supposed to symbolise the passion of Christ. The ten sepals represent the apostles, the dark centre the crown of thorns, the five stamens the wounds, the three styles the nails, and the leaves the hands of the persecutors.

It originates from South America. Alkaloids in the leaves reduce blood pressure.

Wild Passionfruit or Pok Pok (*Passiflora foetida*) is a common vine at lower altitudes. It has similar but smaller flowers, enclosed in a net of feathery green bracts, which open early in the morning.

Water Lemon or Pomn dilyann (*Passiflora laurifolia*) is a woody climber with leathery leaves fourteen centimetres (six inches) long and large, spectacular purple and white flowers, ten centimetres (four inches) wide. Its oval, yellowish fruit, eight centimetres (three inches) long, contains edible pulp.

Previous page: Top: Wild Passionfruit, bottom left: Passion Flower, bottom right: Water Lemon

PETREA
Petrea volubilis

An ornamental climbing shrub which bears sprays of purplish blue flowers, the sepals are lighter in colour than the petals and outlast them.

The plant originates from Central America. Other names include Blue Petrea, Purple Wreath Vine, Queen's Wreath, and Lilac. The genus is named after the famous English plant-lover, Lord Petre.

The tough stems are sometimes used to make 'ropes' (*volubilis* means 'twining').

Illustrated on following page

PITCHER PLANT (Lalyann potao)
Nepethnes pervillei

Unique to Seychelles, the Pitcher Plant is common on Mahé and Silhouette in high rocky areas. The thick, leathery leaves develop climbing tendrils or green and russet pitchers up to fifteen centimetres (six inches) tall, with lids. It has small yellow flowers, with separate male and female plants.

Insects are attracted to a sugary secretion on the inner walls of the pitcher. Once inside they slip into the liquid in the base, which digests them. Despite this, the larvae of certain mosquitoes live inside the pitchers.

There are about seventy species of pitcher plant worldwide, of which all but the Seychelles and Madagascar species are Oriental. Some authorities consider the Seychelles' species to belong to a separate genera, *Anurosperma*.

Illustrated on previous page

RANGOON CREEPER (Lalyann vermifuz)
Quisqualis indica

This lowland, semi-climbing shrub, with thorns and colourful bunches of about ten tubular pink or red flowers, originates from the Far East. In Seychelles, the fruits, roots, and leaves are used medicinally hence the local name 'vermifuz' meaning worm-expelling.

Illustrated on following page

SKY FLOWER
Thunbergia grandiflora

A vigorous climbing plant which often reaches more than nine metres (thirty feet) high, draping downwards over trees and wires. The flowers vary from white to dark-blue, but most commonly, pale-blue. Five petals surround a yellowish white throat. Other names include Blue Trumpet and Sky Vine. It originates from India.

VANILLA ORCHID (Lavannir maron)
Vanilla phalaenopsis

Possibly the most beautiful of Seychelles' unique flowers, its thick, green, leafless stems sprawl over small trees or granite rocks. Slender aerial roots branch to the sides. The large white flowers, reminiscent of daffodils, have an inner trumpet with a peach-coloured throat. The flowers, which bloom one at a time only after heavy rain, fading by about noon, grow in clusters. They produce pods, but these render no vanillin.

Previous page: Top: Sky Flower. Bottom: Vanilla Orchid.

5. LILIES

CANNA LILY
Canna sp.

At first glance, this common garden ornamental resembles a gladioli. The showy flowers vary in colour, the most common forms being combinations of yellow, orange, or red. Large, spear-shaped leaves grow from the base of the plant. What appear to be petals are really modified stamens, only one producing pollen.

It originates from South America. The rhizomes of some species are eaten or used to produce an arrowroot starch.

Illustrated on following page

FLOWER OF THE WEST WIND (Krokus)
Zephyranthes candida

A common ornamental, this plant has narrow, grass-like leaves and bears solitary white flowers, five centimetres (two inches) across, which resemble crocuses. As its other names, Rain Lily and Thunder Lily imply, it flowers after rain. In Seychelles, this means it can flower at any time of year but it is most noticeable during the North-West Monsoon. There is also a yellow variety.

The related species, Pink Rain Lily (*Zephyranthes rosea*) has thicker leaves and pink flowers. The family originates from America.

Previous page: Top: Flower of the West Wind,
Bottom: Pink Rain Lily

SEYCHELLES LILY (Lis Dipei)
Crinum amabile

This spectacular *crinum* has long stalks with clusters of up to twenty trumpet-shaped flowers of ten centimetres (four inches). The petals are white, with a candy pink stripe down the centre. It grows in open areas near the sea, and in gardens.

Although, despite its name, this plant is not unique to Seychelles, it is a prominent feature of the coastal flora of many islands, especially La Digue and Desroches.

Illustrated on following page

SPIDER LILY (Lis bel-d-nwit)
Hymenocallis littoralis

Related to the *crinums*, this species grows in drier areas, and is often seen at the top of beaches. It is a native of tropical America. As the local name suggests, the flowers open towards evening and give off a pleasant fragrance. The flowering stalk has long tubes, each with a funnel-shaped white flower and long spidery segments. The green stamens, with orange anthers, protrude from the tube.

Illustrated on previous page

GINGERS (Zingembre)

WILD GINGER
Hedychium flavescens

This is a cultivated and escaping plant with fragrant pale-yellow flowers. Since antiquity ginger has been one of the most important trade items of the Far East, valued for its medicinal uses. The roots, which die when exposed to sunlight, resemble the human digestive tract.

Ginger tea is soothing at the onset of a cold or sore throat, aids the digestion, and stimulates the appetite. Ginger also relieves diarrhoea, nausea, gout, toothache, and is used as an aphrodisiac and breath-freshener.

It has many culinary uses — as a condiment, flavouring, sweetmeat, and for marmalade.

TORCH GINGER
Amomum magnificum

An ornamental ginger which produces a large spike bearing a spectacular pink conical head of flowers surrounded by a circle of stiff pink bracts.

Previous page. Top: Wild Ginger. Bottom: Torch Ginger

CREPE GINGER
Costus speciosus

This variety has spiral stems and erect clusters of red bracts with large white flowers. It is also known as White Costus and Spiral Ginger. In Greek, 'costus' means a spicy, pepper-like root, and in Latin an Indian shrub that yields a valuable ointment. Unlike most gingers, it has no aroma, but contains the steroid, *diosgenin*, which is used in the production of sex hormones. It is a native of India.

OSTRICH PLUME GINGER
Alpinia purpurata

Also known as Red Ginger, this plant bears an erect spike of waxy red bracts with less striking white flowers. It is a native of Malaysia.

SHELL GINGER
Alpinia zerumbet

Growing up to three metres (ten feet) high, this plant produces showy flowering stems thirty centimetres (one foot) long. The individual, waxy white flowers have a yellow lip spotted and striped with red.

The root is used medicinally and as a flavouring, but it is bitter, containing one per cent ethereal oils. It originates from South China.

Following page: Top left: Crepe Ginger, Top Right: Ostrich Plume Ginger, Bottom: Shell Ginger

HANGING HELICONIA
Heliconia rostrata

The genus *Heliconia* is named after Mount Helicon, abode of the Greek muses and sacred to Apollo. It is native to tropical America and is related to bananas, having very similar leaves.

The plant is distinguished by its hanging spike of bracts, usually red, containing yellow flowers.

Illustrated on previous page

PARROT'S PLANTAIN
Heliconia psittacorum

This related species grows up to one metre (three feet) and has long stalked leaves and a flowering, zigzag spike with thin, orange bracts and erect yellow flowers with greenish black tips.

Illustrated on following page

LOBSTER CLAW (Mordan krab)
Heliconia bihai

Another species of *Heliconia*, this bears an erect flattened spike of boat-shaped, bright crimson bracts with green edges. The bracts contain green flowers.

Because of their bright colours, unusual shape, and ability to last for up to two weeks, the cuttings are popular in flower arrangements.

Illustrated on previous page

LANTANA (Vyeyfiy)
Lantana camara

A low, scrambling shrub with small spines on the woody stems and hairy, toothed leaves, it bears umbrella-like clusters of small tubular flowers of varying colours. The pink, yellow, and white form, found growing wild in Seychelles along roadsides, pathways, and open areas, is the most common. There is also an orange form, common in hotel gardens, and occasionally you may see a purple form.

The fruits are like small blackcurrants. The pounded leaves are used to treat wounds and ulcers. They also make a stimulating tea. As it has few insect enemies and is shunned by cattle, lantana is a serious weed in some countries. The plant originates from tropical America.

Illustrated on following page

PORTULACA (Gorz torti)
Portulaca grandiflora

This common garden plant with fleshy leaves 2.5 centimetres
(one inch) long, bears colourful flowers, both double or single,
of white, yellow, gold, pink, red and purple. It is found
throughout the tropics.

Illustrated on previous page

STAR OF BETHLEHEM (Lerb pwazon)
Laurentia longiflora

A very common plant on shady roadsides, up to thirty centimetres (one foot) high, with long, toothed leaves, and white, star-like flowers growing from tubular stems, it is extremely poisonous. Its previous scientific name, 'hippobroma' means 'horse poison'. The juice of the plant causes inflammation of the skin and eyes and may lead to blindness. It originates from Southern USA and South America.

Illustrated on following page

TROPICBIRD ORCHID (Payanke)
Angraecum eburneum

The national flower of Seychelles, indigenous to the country, this orchid, with fleshy leaves and a curving stem about sixty centimetres (two feet) long, bears white flowers five centimetres (two inches) across, with a long spur of fifteen centimetres (six inches). Reminiscent of the graceful Tropicbird, the flower is a favourite for bridal bouquets.

Illustrated on previous page

VERVAINS (Zepi ble)

NETTLE-LEAVED VERVAIN (Zepi ble)
Stachytarpheta urticifolia

A common, erect woody herb with oval, serrated leaves and a flowering spike up to one metre (three feet) high. The deep-blue flowers grow directly from the central spike, only a few flowers opening at a time.

JAMAICAN VERVAIN (Zepi ble ke-d-rat)
Stachytarpheta jamaicensis

Unlike Nettle-leaved Vervain, this similar but smaller plant, more prostrate and with a much paler blue flower, is usually confined to coastal areas.

CHANGEABLE VERVAIN (Zepi ble ros)
Stachytarpheta mutabilis

Another similar plant with pinkish red flowers, it is much less common than the other two species.

Following page, Top: Nettle-leaved Vervain,
Bottom Left: Jamaican Vervain, Bottom Right: Changeable Vervain

WATER HYACINTH
Eichhornia crassipes

This aquatic ornamental and escaping herb has long, feathery roots, round, fleshy leaves, and candles of lilac and pale-blue flowers, the throats of which are streaked with yellow. It originates from tropical America.

Inflated leafstalks enable the plant to float. After it was introduced on the Upper Nile rafts of plants became a considerable hazard, spreading as much as 1.4 kilometres (0.8 miles) a day upstream, and 2.5 kilometres (1.5 miles) downstream, blocking irrigation pumps, delaying steamers, and increasing the incidence of malaria and bilharzia.

Illustrated on previous page

YELLOW ALDER (Koket)
Turnera ulmifolia

Also known as Holy Rose, this is a common plant found along paths, roadsides, and in coconut plantations throughout Seychelles from sea level to middle altitudes. It is a herb with yellow flowers five centimetres (two inches) that close by midday. The hairy, serrated leaves are up to fifteen centimetres (six inches) long. It originates from South America and is used medicinally in Seychelles.

Illustrated on following page

YUCCA
Yucca aloifolia

This ornamental plant, with spikes of stiff green leaves about sixty centimetres (two feet) long, has a central flowering spike that bears many pendulous white flowers. These are boiled and served as salad. Other names include Spanish Bayonet and Adam's Needle.

In their native Mexico, Yuccas have a fascinating symbiotic relationship with certain species of moth, the larvae of which feed on the developing Yucca seeds. To make sure of the food supply, the female moth gathers the pollen into balls and takes it to another flower. Placing the ball carefully on the stigma, she then lays her eggs in the ovary of the flower.

When the eggs hatch, the larvae feed on the young seeds, but leave most untouched. Finally the larvae burrow out of the developing fruit and fall to the ground. Yucca fruits often display the scars of this exit.

The moth and plant are interdependent. The Yucca needs the moth to ensure pollination, and the moth needs the Yucca for food.

Illustrated on previous page

INDEX

Page 123: Canna Lily. Following pages: Spikes of golden yellow flowers crown the Yellow Flame, source of a prized batik dye. Page 128: Colourful sprays of Bougainvillea comprise bracts which conceal the tiny white flowers.